BETRAYED BY TRUTHS

TRUTH OR LIES BOOK 2

ELLA MILES

D1614489

FREE BOOKS

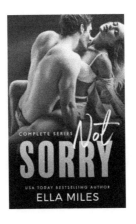

Read **Not Sorry** for **FREE**! And sign up to get my latest releases, updates, and more goodies here→EllaMiles.com/freebooks

Follow me on BookBub to get notified of my new releases and recommendations here→Follow on BookBub Here

Join Ella's Bellas FB group to grab my **FREE** book **Pretend I'm Yours**→Join Ella's Bellas Here

TRUTH OR LIES SERIES

PROLOGUE

ENZO

MY EYES OPEN BEFORE DAWN. Not because I'm an early riser or enjoy watching the sunrise. But out of necessity —survival.

My feet hit the ground before my body is fully awake. My senses put out feelers in every direction, trying to determine any threat before it ends me. I pull the gun from under my pillow and aim it around the room. I no longer sleep without it. Not after my father's last "test" left me fighting off a dozen men with nothing but my thirteen-year-old body's scrawny muscles to defend myself.

I still my breathing and heartbeat as I focus. But I know immediately there is no one in my bedroom but me. The room is silent and dark.

I put my gun in the back of my jeans. *Yes, I sleep in jeans.* I've gotten too many early wake-up calls needing me to be ready to fight. And I'd rather fight with pants on than in my boxers. My junk feels better protected with another layer of clothes on, even if in the end it makes no difference.

I grab the black T-shirt that lies on the chair in the corner of my room and pull it over my head before stepping into my work boots. Then I slink to the window, thumb the drapes open just enough to see out through the thin slit in the fabric to the early morning sky. The sun is hovering on the horizon bringing with it the light.

I let the drapes fall closed, and then move with silent feet through the house—through corridors and down staircases. Through the house I will inherit someday when I become the king of evil incarnate and take over from my father.

Demolishing the house will be the first thing I do when I take over. I hate this fucking house. I hate its thick brick walls. The cold, drafty hallways that weren't built to accommodate air conditioning. The gargoyle statues that seem from another time, not meant to stare out over the seas of Miami. It's like my father lifted this house from medieval France and plopped it on a hillside in Florida. It's completely out of place here among the rows of beach houses.

And to me, it feels like a prison I have no hope of ever escaping.

I stumble to an abrupt stop when I reach the kitchen. My father's eyes sear into mine, and I know my fate from the way his nostrils flare at the sight of me.

"What are you fucking doing? You think you deserve to eat breakfast before even putting in an hour's work?" he asks, lifting a cup of coffee to his lips.

Yes, I fucking need to eat breakfast! I don't know how he expects me to pack on muscle if I never get to eat.

I don't say that. It might make me feel better for a second, but in the end, it would earn me a beating.

"Just awaiting your orders, sir."

That pisses him off more. *Dammit, what did I say?*

Father stands from the stool he's been sitting on while,

waiting for me to make a mistake. His grip on the mug tightens until it shatters and hot coffee spills from the broken mug. The liquid must burn my father's skin, but he doesn't notice nor care.

I eye the broken shards, knowing my father could use it as a weapon against me at any second. I count the pieces preparing for an attack.

But I should know better than to think my father would be predictable.

Instead, he marches to me with all his furry behind him. Oozing from his pores as steam shoots from his nose. His face darkens to a shade of red that can only be used to describe the devil. All he's missing are horns and pitchfork.

"Awaiting orders?" He reaches for my neck, a move he's done countless times. I escape with ease, darting around to the other side of the kitchen island.

"Awaiting fucking orders?! Really, Enzo? Have you learned nothing from all our years of training! No son of mine awaits fucking orders. You give them! You rule them! You never take them!"

My father launches himself at me before I can escape. I may be quick, but he has years of experience, thick muscles, and more rage than I ever thought one man could contain behind him—while I live in fear.

He pins me against the cabinet with his forearm shoved against my neck, and his leg shoving hard into my stomach. He grabs my gun and quickly disarms me, tossing it to the floor behind him.

I'm powerless. He could kill me right now, and there is nothing I could do about it.

He won't. He needs me.

That's what I keep reminding myself every day.

I can't die. He can't kill me.

But sometimes, in the gloomy pain that encompasses my every day, I wish he would. Eternal sleep has to be easier than the torture I go through every day just to survive.

I don't flinch as his fist pounds into the side of my head. I jolt into the cabinet ensuring a dent in the wood as my head makes contact. The familiar taste of blood coats my mouth, but I don't think he knocked any teeth out this time.

Who needs coffee when you have dear old father to jolt you awake with a good morning jab to the face?

"Look at me, son."

I whip my head back to face him with nothing but disdain.

Dad sighs, exhaling his frustration, coffee, and whiskey. He may have just been drinking coffee, but I know his day is wrapping to a close, not starting. He was out late last night, chasing down a yacht from one of our enemies who threatened his control of the seas. From the anger waving off of him, the chase didn't go well. But my father returned, and the only way that would have happened would be if he eliminated the bastard for daring to kill a single crew member from our ranks.

He shakes his head as he peers into my broken eyes. "Do you want to become Black?"

I nod my head, knowing any other answer will land me another blow to the head. Although, I'm not sure I want to become Black. Black is synonymous with my father. And he's the last person I want to become.

"Then you have to put in the work. The Millers will be preparing their heir to take over. To defeat you. He will be stronger than any foe you've ever faced. You can't lose."

I squint my eyes. My father would never allow me to come home if I lost. Good thing he'll be dead when it's finally time for me to do battle. That's what triggers the next

Black to take his place. And I can't imagine a world where my father will ever die. So I don't expect to face my opponent until I'm ninety.

"You will be Black. The legend, the myth, the ruler. You will take my place someday. And when that day comes, you'll be more dangerous and ruthless than I ever was. You have a better teacher than I did. You will be more prepared to take over than any heir before you."

If this is what I have to do to prepare, then I don't want to be Black. I don't want any part of it. I'd rather lose and live my life on the sea, learning how to sail, and working hard than go through another day of my father's training course.

"And when you become king, like me, you will be free."

Free.

He said the magic word.

The one thing I crave more than anything—*freedom*.

My father grins, his eyes deepening as if he unlocked the key to the greatest treasure, instead of just finding the key to getting me to take his training seriously.

"Good," he says releasing me.

I ball my hands into fists, instead of reaching for my pounding head like I want. *Never show weakness.* I learned that lesson when I was seven and cried when I skinned my knee on the sidewalk after riding my bike too fast. Father whipped me for every tear I shed, which only made me cry harder and earn more lashings. When my tears had finally dried up, I had changed. I've never cried since that day. I'll never cry again.

Never flinch.

Never wince.

Never cry.

I am invincible. At least that is what the world thinks of me. I'm unstoppable.

His lips curl up higher as the evil wheels in his brain turn with an idea.

Fuck me.

I'm screwed.

Last time he had an idea, I was forced to run barefoot through the forest behind the house. I ran for three days straight with him hunting me on horseback with the promise that if he caught me, he'd shoot me.

My stomach lurches thinking of what happened when he finally caught up to me. My feet were bleeding; my body was frail from not eating; I was delirious with dehydration. He should have been proud that I lasted for three days. I hadn't slept or eaten. I never stopped moving. It took him three whole days to track me down and find me. He had the advantage of horses, scent dogs, and a weapon.

But father wasn't proud. I don't know how long he expected me to last or if shooting me was the plan the entire time no matter what I did. But my shoulder will never be the same.

He shot me without a word—only a dark stare of disappointment.

I was in shock, so I didn't realize what had happened until he motioned for me to follow.

I took one step and collapsed from the pain. When I awoke, I expected to be in a hospital or at least in my bed at home. Instead, I found myself covered in dirt, my shoulder still bleeding from the wound my father caused.

I could have died!

The bastard.

But I can't die. So I pulled myself up and walked home. Father wasn't there when I arrived, but I knew better at that point than to call a doctor. So I called Langston, one of my best friends. His father is a doctor, so I thought he could help. But all he could do was pull out the bullet, wash it clean with vodka, and then force the vile liquid down my throat until I passed out again to avoid the pain.

My shoulder still throbs six months later. That's when I started keeping a gun under my pillow. That's when any spare moment I have I'm practicing shooting or deflecting. I will not let any man shoot me again. Not without fighting back.

"Come," my father says like I'm a dog as he walks away from me.

I take the moment to inspect my head, but I don't find any contusion, bump, or blood. Probably just another concussion to add to the endless list of pain my father has caused me.

He picks up my gun before I have the chance.

Fuck.

I straighten my spine. *I will not let him shoot me again.*

Although, that's what I feel like I'm walking into. A shooting range where I'll be the target.

We descend down more stairs, and the prickling on the back of my neck tells me exactly where we are going—*the dungeon.*

My father doesn't hold very many men prisoner. And the ones he does he doesn't keep for very long. But there are a few rooms on the premise for this very purpose. To hold dangerous men, torture them, and then kill them when he gets the information he requires.

I swallow down the fear that begins to rise with each step.

We pass door after door of cages meant to loosen tongues into speaking, and then we stop at the last door. My father takes a key from his pocket and opens the door to the darkness. I already know what awaits me.

Nothing.

Blackness.

Loneliness.

This won't be a test of physical pain; it will be mental as all of his most ruthless tests are.

I don't wait for him to tell me what to do. I don't take orders. *Ha.* He forces me to take orders every single day.

But one day, I won't.

I'm already starting to get big enough that I can imagine a day when I'll have enough muscles and skills that I won't have to follow my father's orders. Except he has the power of the entire Surrender crew behind him. Most men in Miami would follow his every order just to stay alive or earn a favor from the notorious Black.

I walk into the cold, damp room. When I turn I see my father's smirk on his face. He doesn't want me to follow any orders, except his. He wants me to be his puppet he can control, even from the grave.

He tosses my gun into the room. I watch as it lands on the dirty floor at my feet.

Maybe I was wrong? Why the hell do I need a gun if he's just going to lock me in the room for a few days?

"This is a test of patience and self-control," he says.

I bend down and pick up the gun, not taking my eyes off of my father and my senses going on high alert.

"Why the gun?" I ask as he closes the door.

He grins, with a wicked glare. "Because before I open this door, you'll want to kill yourself rather than survive through one more minute of the pain. And you need to learn self-control, self-preservation. You need to prefer pain to death."

The door latches with a loud thud. Locking me in for longer than I ever want to imagine.

This should be an easy test for me. I have more patience than my father. I thrive on being alone. I can sleep for days uninterrupted and dream of a better world where I don't have to handle endless nights of pain just to show I'm worthy.

Easy.

But my days and nights are anything but.

I don't get food—not even scraps.

And my only choice for water is the occasional trickle that seeps through the walls when it rains that I'm forced to lick from the dirty bricks. I resort to drinking my own pee in hopes of getting the tiniest drops of liquid. But I haven't peed in days.

I've lost track of time. *How many days have passed and how many left to endure?*

My body won't survive much longer. It aches to move, to think, to breathe.

So I don't do anything.

I've even learned to shut off my mind.

I just exist.

And then I see the flicker of the gun that rests in the corner. I could end this.

Yes, that's what I'll do. End this.

I just have to make it to the gun.

Move body, move!

Now that I've made my decision, I want it to end—now.

But I can barely think, let alone move.

Every thought becomes a struggle.

I reach one arm out, then the other. Now pull my body forward as my legs push. I gain an inch. Then another. And another.

Until my fingers brush against the gun.

I smile for the first time in weeks.

This is going to end. I'm going to end it. I'll piss off father, leave him without an heir. That thought alone sparks my happiness. My final act won't be to kill my father, but myself. That will enrage him more than anything else ever could.

I grasp the gun and put it to my head.

My hands are shaky, but it doesn't matter if I miss the center of my head as long as I hit some part of my body. I'm too weak to handle a gunshot. I'll die from blood loss within minutes. It will just prolong my agony.

I keep my eyes open staring into the dark abyss, and then I pull the trigger.

CLICK.

Shit.

I remove the gun from my head and pull again.

Nothing.

The bastard removed the fucking bullets.

I fling the gun towards the wall, but my arms are too weak for it to even reach it. The metal falls to the dirt with a soft thud.

That's when the door flies open, and my father's chuckles fill the room.

"You failed. You're weak. I think it's time I teach you a lesson."

I should speak. Tell him how strong I am for surviving as long as I did, but my voice doesn't even work. Nothing does.

I know he's kicking my stomach because my body jars, but I don't feel it. I've shut out the world—the darkness. Even though I'm not dead, I feel dead. I'm gone.

More kicks, punches, and whips. I feel blood oozing, my body moving, but I don't fight back. I have nothing left.

"You're a fucking piece of worthless shit. I didn't raise a coward, a fucking pussy. Get up! Fight back!"

I can't.

You try to fight when you've been starved for weeks.

And then I see it—*my salvation.*

I see the glimmer from his knife sticking from beneath his pant leg. But he's stopped kicking me, instead preferring punches.

So I turn to him and spit my frustration.

His face turns to steely rage. And I brace as his foot makes contact. I ignore the force and grab his leg holding on for long enough to grab the knife, and then I stab hard into his foot.

I know the jab isn't deep, given the tough leather of his boot, but it's enough to make contact. *Enough to end this.*

My father doesn't make a sound at the pain he's in. His impervious armor is up all around him as always.

But he stops the torture.

"Pick yourself up," he says.

I summon everything inside me to get myself to stand.

He smirks in approval.

"Maybe you'll earn the right to call yourself Black after all." And then he's gone.

I smirk. I won. My first win against this monster. It feels good. And if I can win once, I can win again and again. Until I'm free.

1

KAI

WHAT THE HELL did I just agree to?

I stare across at Enzo, who is more my enemy than I ever realized. *How could I not know that I had a claim to an empire?*

This house, the money Enzo's acquired, the resources, the men—they could have all been mine as easily as they are his.

I didn't have to grow up thinking I had no choices, no chances at ever becoming something more. I could have had everything—all the money I could ever spend. I still can.

But only if I beat Enzo—at a game I don't even understand.

A game where only the strongest win. I don't even know if I will survive the tests, I'm so weak.

But I want to play. It may be my only chance to truly be free.

Archard, Enzo's lawyer, reenters as if he has been listening to our entire conversation and knows now is the time to arrange things.

Westcott appears too, carrying a chair for Archard,

because apparently, this conversation is going to last longer than the previous time he was here and stood watching us.

Archard sits in the chair Westcott provides. Westcott looks to Enzo who simply nods, and Westcott leaves us.

"So it appears the two of you have agreed to the terms of the contract," Archard says.

Enzo doesn't respond; he just glares into my soul waiting for me to back out or change my mind. So I answer, "Yes, although I'd like to know a little more about the contract."

"Of course, Miss Miller. We have lots to discuss."

Archard retrieves the large pile of papers from the center of the table. And then pulls two more stacks from his briefcase. "These are copies of the contract between your two families for you to keep," he says, passing a stack to each me and Enzo.

Enzo nods but barely glances at the papers. It's clear he's seen them before, while I grasp onto them like they are my lifeline to a past and future I don't understand.

"This contract was written to ensure Surrender, and all of its entities, go to the proper heir. *The true heir.* The one capable of running the organization properly," Archard says.

"Surrender? You mean the club? The winner only gets the club?" I ask.

"No, Surrender is one of many clubs and entities the winner, or heir apparent, will control. I'm sure Mr. Rinaldi will give you a tour of everything you could inherit. Surrender is also the name of the umbrella company that encompasses everything," Archard pauses.

Enzo, or Mr. Rinaldi as Archard called him, tightens his lip and gives the slightest of nods.

"But according to the records here," Archard flips a page

before continuing to read. "The winner will receive ownership of sixty-five bars and clubs, ten superyachts, and seven estates. The winner will also be given control of the entire organization including the over a thousand employees that work for Surrender and encompassing companies that include bars, clubs, yachts, and security."

My eyes widen with every word.

"The winner will be given the power to a ten billion dollar organization that runs Miami and most of the sea between here and the Bahamas," Enzo says with a threatening tone in his deep baritone voice. He steeples his hand on the table as if this is an ordinary day, a regular meeting —not one deciding our destiny, the fates of over a thousand employees, and the status of the underground of Miami.

But it's clear from Enzo's expression he doesn't think I can do this. Even if I were to win, I couldn't run the empire properly.

"So if I win, I get everything?" I ask.

Archard nods. "Yes, you would have the keys to the world. You would never want again. You would have more money than you could ever spend—more power than most kings. But you also need to understand how serious the power you would gain controls. You would take the lives of thousands of people into your hands. You would be responsible for ensuring Surrender, the name of the organization, not just the club, continues to grow and thrive. You would be responsible for ensuring the company continued to be profitable. And the clients that hire Surrender for protection are ruthless. If you fucked up, they would come for your head. Becoming Mr. or Miss Black is a dangerous job. One you shouldn't take lightly."

I let it sink in. All that I stand to gain if I win. I would obtain money, power, control. But I would also inherit danger, darkness, cruelty. I would acquire everything I hate.

Maybe I could change it?

Somehow I don't think you can change a criminal organization overnight.

"And what does the loser get?" I ask, because I have to know. I'm much more likely to lose. I wasn't prepared for a life of power.

"Nothing," Archard says with thinned lips.

Nothing.

I won't be any better off than I am now. I have nothing to gain by playing, except maybe my freedom from this house.

"Shall I continue?" Archard asks again looking to Enzo for permission.

My rage rises, although it shouldn't. Archard is Enzo's lawyer. He works for him, of course he would ask him the questions. But I want to be looked at like I have a chance to win this too.

"If Miss Miller is ready to continue," Enzo bounces the attention back to me.

I try my best to smile to rid myself of the negative feelings. "Yes, let's continue."

Archard flips the page, and I do the same with the papers in front of me.

"Let's discuss the rules."

Rules.

I glance to Enzo expecting him to be studying the paper in front of him, but instead, he's studying me.

I shift nervously in my seat, wishing on some level I could be having this meeting alone with Archard, instead of getting unnerved by Enzo's constant gaze. But on the other hand, I welcome the heat pouring off Enzo. It both calms and excites me.

"The first term is that only one person from the new generation can compete. The oldest direct heir gets the right to decide if they compete or if someone else from the same generation is better suited for the task and job at hand. Now is the only time to swap out for someone different. If there is a different sibling, cousin, etc. from this generation you would rather have compete from your family for the name of Black and all that comes with it, let it be known now," Archard says.

"I don't have any siblings or cousins. It's just me," I say.

Archard turns to Enzo, although I would guess he already knows his answer. This is just a formality.

Does Enzo have any siblings or cousins he fought first to earn this right?

"I will be the one competing," Enzo says blankly.

"Good, now let's discuss how a winner will be determined," Archard says.

I stare down at the next page where Archard begins reading.

"There will be five rounds to determine who can claim the name Black. The first person to win three rounds will become the winner."

Five rounds. That doesn't seem so bad.

"The first and third round rules were determined by Miss Miller's father."

I raise my eyebrows. *Dad? He determined two of the games?*

My heart aches. *Why didn't you tell me about this Dad? You could have prepared me to fight. To win.* Instead, you left me in the dark. *Did you even choose a game I could win or did you expect me to lose as quickly as possible?*

"The second and fourth games were determined by Mr. Rinaldi's father."

I gulp as I look across to the darkest man I know. If his father won the games before, then I expect him to be even crueler than the man in front of me. Which means whatever games he chose, I'm fucked.

"And the final game, if needed, was determined by both fathers."

They had to agree? What game would they agree to? I doubt our families would agree on anything if they've been doing battle for generations—where the winner gets to live like a king, and the loser barely survives in a trailer park. No wonder we struggled so much.

What else did you hide from me dear old Dad?

I need to find my father. He has some serious explaining to do.

"The winner of each round should be easy to determine. There is no subjection to the games. There is a clear winner or loser as determined by the rules of each game. But if a winner needs to be decided, or a rule determined to be won or broken, I'm the one to make such decision."

"*You?* Wouldn't that give Enzo an unfair advantage since you work for him?" I ask.

"No, Miss Miller, my loyalty lies with the Surrender organization and the man or woman who claims the title of Black. As Mr. Rinaldi no longer holds that title, I have no loyalty to him," Archard says.

I frown. I don't like this one bit. It feels rigged.

Enzo smirks as my reaction. "Don't worry, Miss Miller."

I hate when he calls me by my last name.

"You'll soon learn this game is the epitome of fair," Enzo continues.

I snark. He means these games will be anything but fair. But that's the point. Surrender isn't run fairly. This life, this world isn't. I of all people understand that.

Archard ignores our exchange. "The games begin upon the demise of the previous Mr. Black. As he died three years ago, that means the games should start immediately."

I suspected Enzo's father was dead, but this confirms it.

Enzo doesn't react to Archard's words. He doesn't get emotional at the thought of his father being dead. I don't know what that means, but I suspect he didn't have any better relationship with his father than I did with mine. At least his father was honest about him about this world.

I wonder how his father died, but neither Enzo nor Archard explain. I don't know how old his father was or what his health condition was like, but if what Archard said was true, even the winner is at risk of dying young. Black may have all the riches of the world, but also the enemies. It's a dangerous job.

Do I even want to become the next Black? I would have to do the job. Be ruthless. Order people dead to protect my own. *Could I do such a thing?*

I stare at Enzo across from me. Tall, dark, handsome. But also merciless, powerful, God-like. He's muscle, steel, and strength.

He was bred for this.

Trained for this.

He's been doing the job for the last three years. He was brought up by a father who won and knew what it would take to continue to win.

While I grew up in a trailer park with nothing.

No mother. Barely a father.

No money.

No food.

No energy to form muscles needed to fight.

No guns to wield as weapons to learn how to fire. And

after being broken by the worst of men, I'm even weaker than before. I have no chance of winning. *None.*

This battle is worse than the odds of David and Goliath. David did win, but that was fictional. This is real—and I won't bet on me winning.

"When do we find out what the games are? When will they take place?" I ask.

"You will be given at least twenty-four-hours notice of when and where each game will take place along with any items you need to complete the task. Your fathers determined the rules of each game and when the rules of the game will be revealed. The first game rules, as determined by your father Miss Miller, will not be revealed until the game starts," Archard says.

Fucking father. He couldn't even give me a warning to allow me a day or two to prepare for his stupid game. Unless the game is surviving the longest without food, I have no chance of winning.

I might as well surrender now. The sooner I lose, the sooner Enzo might let me leave. The sooner I will be free.

"When does the first game start? Is this our twenty-four-hour warning to the first game?" I ask.

"First, I need you both to sign, agreeing you are the heirs who will be playing, and then I will set everything in motion. It will take a day or two at least to get things sorted, and then I will notify you both twenty-four-hours before the first round. This isn't that warning."

Archard slides the papers to me. I sign below my name I wrote practically in crayon when I was five and agreed one person from my generation would fight.

Except I'm the only one from my generation. I'm the only chance the Millers have of winning.

I slide the paper across to Enzo. He signs and then glances to the door behind him.

Langston and Zeke enter.

I frown. I'm sure they were listening to everything as well. *Why does he get henchmen to help him while I get nothing?*

"Sir, there is a situation at Surrender," Zeke says.

Enzo nods. "I'll be right there."

"No," Archard answers.

We all freeze.

Archard turns to Enzo. "You are no longer Black. You should have never claimed the title to begin with. You no longer get to make any decisions or wield any power."

"But the organization can't run for days or weeks or months or however long this fucking farce lasts. I will be the winner anyway. Isn't there some clause in there about who runs the organization while the heir is decided?" Enzo snarls.

"Yes, you are required to run it together," Archard says.

Together.

I silently laugh. *Good luck with getting us to agree on anything.*

But the way Enzo is staring at me, I think he wants to do a lot more than run an empire together. He wants to slam our bodies together, and he wouldn't be giving me any control in the matter. I would have to surrender my body to him.

"Come on then, we have an empire to run," Enzo snarls.

2

ENZO

The contract is signed.

I never thought this day would come—the end.

I thought I'd be forever trapped in a lie I could never escape. I thought pretending Kai was dead would save me. I thought not having a Miller line to fight for their right to the throne would have satisfied me.

Instead, it made me restless.

I didn't earn my position.

I was given it.

But now, I can claim it rightfully.

You hear that, Dad?! In a few weeks, this will all be over, and I'll be the winner. I'm the rightful heir. I will be Black.

I exhale deeply, trying to let go of every drop of discomfort my father caused me over the years—the pushing, torture, ruthlessness. I should let every painful feeling go.

I can't.

Not until I've won.

Then I can pretend all the suffering I went through was worth it. Then I can prove my father wrong.

Kai Miller may be strong. In fact, she's the most relentless person I've ever met. But unless all five rounds are who can withstand suffering the longest, she has no chance of winning. Even if I hadn't trained my entire life for this job.

Her chances are hopeless.

I could have prepared hard for a year and still beat her. Not because she's a woman, but because of the last six years. Her body is badly beaten and still recovering. She barely has enough fat covering her bones, let alone real muscle. And despite being capable of doing whatever it takes to survive, she's still too kind to do this job.

Kai would only ever kill in self-defense, not because it was necessary for the greater good of the organization.

She would never take from those less than her.

Never yell or demonstrate her power to show her strength.

Kai has a heart, even if she keeps it locked away behind a metal cage.

I'm heartless.

My father made sure of that years ago. I'm the only one merciless enough to do the job.

But what will happen to Kai when she loses?

She'll go back to the trailer park with her father. Possibly even ask me for a job to keep her afloat until the next generation attempts to take my power.

Blood boils in my veins at another generation having to face what Kai and I have been through, all to play a stupid game where the winner wins everything and the loser is lucky enough to be left alive.

I stare at the gorgeous woman across from me. Jean shorts hang off her hip bones engulfing her thin legs that I can only imagine will strengthen and tone with time. The spaghetti strapped shirt drapes loosely over her breasts that have started to fill out again. The weight she has gained has begun going to all of my favorite places on her body—her breasts and ass. Her jet black hair reaches far too long down her back in uneven tendrils.

But her physical looks aren't what make her beautiful. I'm sure with more self-care, a beautician, and hair cut, Kai would be a knockout. Her thin frame makes her every supermodel's dream body. But I've had models before; actresses, strippers, every kind of attractive woman.

Kai is gorgeous because of her piercing green-blue eyes. The color sucks me in every time she looks at me. And behind the eyes that trap me is her spirit. The part of her that signed the papers without surrendering, even though she knows her chances of winning are less than one percent.

Her fight to not only survive, but find something better for herself. Something she deserves. I do not doubt that whatever the outcome, she will find what she's looking for one day.

And that will be the worst part of winning—losing her.

I could offer her a job to keep her around, but she wouldn't take it.

Give her money and one of my many houses to keep her close to me, but she won't be bought. No matter how poor she is.

Kai Miller is the most independent, self-sufficient, kick-ass woman I've ever met. Even if she doesn't realize it herself yet.

For now, she's mine.

Trapped under my roof.

For now, that's enough.

My cock hardens in my pants, reminding just how much it's not enough. And how I need a new solution. I want her to be mine forever. Not because I love her and want to make her my wife. But because when I want something, it's mine.

I'm not a monster. I won't take her body by force. She will give it to me willingly, or I won't have her at all.

I cringe thinking about what she's been through. I should set her free of living in my house at least.

But she wouldn't be safe.

Not until I figure out the truth. Because I have an inkling that someone is hunting her after I killed her previous master. Jarod may have been the one who got his hands dirty, but he wasn't the one who owned her.

I head toward the bedroom I've shared with Kai since I stole her for myself. Kai walks silently behind me.

We should be headed to sleep; instead, we are headed out to work in the daylight.

I'm used to going with no sleep—Kai is too. But I don't like her missing any amount of sleep. She needs all the healing powers it can offer her to continue to grow stronger.

I walk to the closet, deciding I'd rather wear jeans and a dark shirt in case whatever emergency we are dealing with is messy. I don't like getting blood on my designer suits.

"What should I wear?" Kai asks.

I freeze and turn to her. "Whatever clothes you can handle."

She frowns crossing her arms. "I can handle wearing clothes."

I smirk. "Since when?"

She huffs. "Since I realized you're a complete asshole and I can't rely on anyone but myself."

My head snaps around looking in her direction as she stomps to her side of the closet and begins pulling her shirt off over her head until her torso is naked like she prefers.

"You think you're tough now? Huh? You think you're done healing?" I ask.

"Yes."

My grin turns evil as I let my dick decide my actions instead of my brain.

I move like a force of wind blowing through the closet. The only thing saving her from my grasp is that I'm so used to not touching her—not having her.

Instead of touching her, the intimidation of my movements pushes her back against the wall, until I box her in with my hands.

I was expecting fear under her pretty eyelashes. Or at least shock.

Instead, she bites her plump lip. Stealing all of my control with one suck.

Fuck.

Her large eyes stare up at me as if waiting to see what I'll do next.

"I'm not afraid of you," she whispers.

"You should be."

"I'm not. I may hate you, but I'm not scared."

Hate.

What does she know about hating me? Because I sold her? That's why she hates me. But I'm keeping her here for her safety. Or at least that's what I keep telling myself.

I could change the hate-filled lust I see in her eyes with one truth. One truth would change her whole perspective on me.

Her hatred for me would vanish with one sentence.

But do I want her hatred gone?

No, it's better if she hates me.

I lean in close, so close the stubble on my face lightly prickles against her cheek. "You're not scared. And you

27

might hate me, but your hatred doesn't prevent you from wanting me. I gave you the best orgasm of your life, and now you want more. Your eyelids are getting heavy at the thought of my cock filling you."

"You will never fuck me," she spits back.

"Not without your permission, no. I'm the devil, but that doesn't make me like *him*," I say, referencing Jarod.

She sucks in a breath.

"You won't fuck me," she says again, to assure herself and me.

I lick my lips and growl low and breathy against her ear, careful not to touch her with any part of me but my breath.

"We'll see," I say as my eyes travel down to her pointed nipples.

Her cheeks pink, but she doesn't hide her breasts from me. She's not embarrassed by her body. And this image of her will sit in my head, stealing my thoughts, the rest of the day.

Damn her.

I won't be able to focus the rest of the day.

She stares down at my cock pressing against my pants.

"We will see," she grins.

I huff.

"Get dressed, Miss Miller, if you would like to accompany me today. We leave in five minutes."

She snarks. "We will leave when I'm ready. As Archard said, you don't get to go anywhere without me."

Fuck the contract. And fuck Archard.

He doesn't control me.

No one does.

Except the fiery woman standing in front of me half-naked. The woman who I could disarm with a brush of my hand because the touch alone would be too much for her.

28

The woman who is the only person who has truly ever stood up to me. Only she is capable of taking me by the balls and leading me wherever she wants.

Luckily for me, she doesn't realize the full depth of her control of me—at least not yet.

"Five minutes, Miss Miller. I'm leaving in five minutes. I extended to you the invitation to ride with me, but if you aren't ready by then, then you are welcome to figure out how to drive yourself in any car you own. Or pay for an Uber with your own money. But if you want a ride from me, I leave in five."

I don't give her a chance to respond.

I leave.

Down the stairs to wait for her.

Sharing a room was a mistake.

Bringing her here was worse.

Letting her sign the contract will be my undoing.

I pace at the bottom of the stairs while I wait for her and try to figure out what I'm going to do with her.

I should have had a dungeon built as my father did; that way I could just lock her up when she pissed me off.

I shake my head.

I won't be a monster.

I will never be that cruel. Even though it's in my blood.

Six minutes later Kai descends the stairs as if to tempt me with leaving. Trying out her newfound power over me as if this is all a game.

It is.

But not one she should be playing. Because she will lose, and the consequences will devastate her.

Kai is wearing dark black pants and a shimmering top that hugs to her skin tighter than anything I've seen on her. Her hair is up in a bun, no longer hiding her face. She must have decided to dress up a little to match me since I never changed out of my suit.

"Is this acceptable to wear, Your Highness?" she asks snakily, knowing she looks hot as hell in this outfit. Men would do what she wants just for a chance to fuck her.

I growl my disapproval in her wearing anything so revealing.

She smiles.

"I think I'll take that as a yes," she says.

"Only if you keep calling me Your Highness. It has a nice ring to it. Maybe I'll have other people start calling me that when I win."

She glares at me. "Don't count me out yet."

I won't.

I would never count Kai Miller out.

"Besides, I did the best I could with limited clothing and no makeup."

I don't want her wearing nice clothes. Or makeup. Or a stylish haircut. It will only make her more attractive to other men. But it's not fair to her. And I'm also a selfish bastard, who wants to see what she would look like dolled up when she dresses to the nines.

"Westcott," I snap, knowing he is waiting down the hallway for any orders I have to give him.

"Yes, Mr. Bla—" he starts and then catches himself as I glare at him.

Kai giggles.

I turn my glare to her, but it doesn't stop her snickering.

"What do you need me to do, sir?" Westcott says instead.

"I need you to talk to Kai and ensure she has everything she needs. Clothing, makeup, a hair stylist. The best of everything on my credit card. Understood?"

"Yes, sir."

Kai's mouth falls open.

"I'll have a stylist stop by later so Kai can choose herself," Westcott says.

I turn to Kai, waiting for her to give her approval, but she's frozen as a statue.

"Kai? Will that work for you? Or would you rather go to a store?" I ask.

She nods instead of answering my questions.

"That will be all, Westcott."

He leaves silently, knowing better than to ask any other questions.

"Let's go. Langston and Zeke already headed to Surrender. There is no telling what mess awaits us." I start toward the driveway where I know Westcott had my car brought out from the garage.

"Um..." she starts.

"What?" I snap. I don't have time for this.

"I have a proposition for you."

I roll my eyes. "I can fuck you later. We need to go, now."

Her eyes darken in defiance. "Do you want to go to Surrender by yourself?"

I stop.

Of course, I do. I don't want to have to babysit her or convince her why we need to do tasks my way.

"What are you proposing?" I ask.

"You go handle the crisis at Surrender."

"And?"

"I go see my father."

My jaw twitches. I want to go to Surrender by myself. But I don't want Kai to go see her father.

It makes sense why she wants to. To find out why he never told her about the deal between the families. And see if she can get him to give her any hints of the tasks he chose.

I understand why. I would want the same myself if I were in her situation.

But I know my answer.

I won't trade or back down.

I don't know why I don't want her going to see her father exactly. I don't trust they will play by the rules, but honestly, I'd prefer it if she knew the first task. It might keep her safe if she was able to practice her skills for a couple of days first and have some sort of plan.

But I don't like sending her to a man who could barely provide her with food. A man who didn't keep her safe. A man I don't trust.

And more importantly, Kai is mine. She lost our truth or lies game. She relinquished herself to me, even if she hasn't let me have her body yet. But I won't share any of the time I have with her. Even with her father. Even if it saves her.

I'm sure I can do my own task efficiently while ensuring she is also safe. That she isn't walking into a trap where another man would hurt her.

"No deal."

"What?" she exclaims.

I start walking to the door, and she scurries after me as we file outside.

"Why not? You don't want me to come. I just want to talk to him. You can send one of your bodyguards to ensure I come back. I just want to know why my father never told me the truth for years."

"No."

Anger flares on her face and despise pulses through her veins. "You don't get to control me anymore. You're not Black. You don't have power over me. I can do what I want."

I snap toward her, reaching my hand out to grab her, unable to resist her skin against mine. I grab her wrist loosely in my hand. The gesture is kind and caring, not like she's my enemy. But the movement is anything but kind. Because she's not prepared for my touch.

I've touched her before, but she's still sensitive to it if she hasn't prepared herself. If I'm being affectionate and lust is flowing through her making her clit throb for me, then she can ignore the panic inside.

Right now she hates me. So she can't escape me.

The touch sends her spiraling to a place she thought she had left. The darkness covers her.

It's cruel.

One of the cruelest things I've ever done to her.

But I can't let her have power.

I can't let her think she has control.

Because if she does, she might think she is free. She might run.

And she has no idea the danger she is in now that she's signed the contract. Word will soon spread that she's the girl who was supposed to be dead come back to life. And all of our enemies will descend thinking of her as a weakness instead of a strength.

I will do my best to keep her hidden. To keep the truth hidden from our enemies. No one needs to know I'm no longer in control and I have to compete against Kai to keep what's mine. But I can't promise our enemies won't find out the truth.

And after what I made her endure before, I won't let her get hurt again. I will protect her the only way I know how.

By fear.

By pain.

By control.

Kai jerks her hand out of my grasp, realizing I'm trying to control her with my touch. "You bastard."

She holds her hand against her chest, away from my reach.

"You're not in control, Kai. You never will be; I know you too well. And I won't let you win—you're mine. Accept it, and I will make your life so much easier."

"And if I don't?"

I pause, letting the wind rustle through us. When it calms, I speak.

"Then you will continue to hate everyone, including yourself."

I beep the car fob and climb into the car, waiting for her to make up her mind. Go back inside or come with me. Because going to see her father isn't an option.

I have more security here than she could ever imagine. Westcott has more skills than she realizes for a fifty-year-old man; he's more security guard than butler.

She will never escape. Not until I determine it's safe.

I owe her that.

She climbs into the passenger side.

"You don't scare me," she repeats her words from earlier.

"I know."

"You won't fuck me."

"I know."

"Then what do you want with me?" she asks.

I press my foot down on the gas, not being gentle as we speed off.

Everything. I want fucking everything.

3

KAI

I STRIDE into Surrender like I own the place.

And I guess technically I do—at least I own it as much as Enzo does. And he walks in like everything and everyone should bow to him as soon as he enters. So I mimic his behavior.

I am strong.

I am fearless.

I am losing my fucking balance in these heels.

Why is it heels are what women are supposed to wear to feel powerful and in control? Why didn't society pick something like tennis shoes, or better yet, furry slippers for women to wear?

But no, society decided women only look hot when balancing on six-inch spikes.

Instead of following Enzo, I walk next to him. Trying my best to look like an equal, instead of his pawn. I don't know where we are going, but I assume Enzo's office.

I was right.

We enter his office and almost immediately there is a knock on the door. We don't even have a chance to speak to each other privately about what our game plan is in dealing with whatever the crisis is.

"Dallas Fell is here to talk about his security. He claims he lost five million dollars because our security entail didn't protect him. He's threatening to kill you and everyone you sent to protect his assets," Langston says poking his head in.

Langston glances from Enzo to me, and it's clear he's worried. This man must be dangerous and pissed at Enzo for failing him.

Enzo just nods like he deals with this every day. He probably does.

"I'm sure he does. Five million is a lot of money to a man like him," Enzo continues.

"Should I send him in?" Langston asks.

"No, we need a few minutes to discuss our game plan first," Enzo says.

"Really? He's irate and causing havoc—flipping tables and shit. I don't think leaving him alone is a good idea," Langston says.

Enzo ignores him as he stares at me. His wheels are obviously turning in a different direction.

"Take him to your office and offer him our best liquor while he waits. Assure Dallas he will have ten million added to his account, and that's what I'm handling while he waits. Then bring him to my office in fifteen minutes," Enzo says, his voice calm and collected.

Ten million! He's going to give this man ten million dollars because he fucked up.

Langston rolls his eyes, and I suspect Enzo acts like this all the time, while Langston is less calm and collected.

"You'll owe me for any damage the asshole does to my office," Langston says.

Enzo smiles tightly. "I always do. Bring Zeke with you. He can rough him up if he gets too out of control."

Langston nods and then leaves.

"Ten million dollars? Don't you think if you are just going to throw that kind of money at someone to fix a problem you should run it by me? That's a fuck ton of money," I say.

"No, it's not a lot of money. Not to *Black*."

I scowl. "It's a lot of money to *me*."

He shakes his head. "Not anymore."

I sigh—he's right. If I win, ten million dollars will be nothing. And if I lose, the money won't be mine anyway.

"Fine."

He grins. "I knew you'd see it my way."

"I do, but from now on run it by me first. I don't want to have to tattle on you to Archard," I smirk.

"You won't tattle on me."

I step closer taking a deep breath as his eyes heat. "I will," I tease.

His eyes drop from my face to my cleavage peeking out from beneath my shirt.

He wants me.

I want him.

And after he brought me to orgasm without so much as touching me, I've been dying to know what it would be like for him to fuck me—but I'm too fucked up for sex.

And I can't get past him selling me.

If I shared my truth would things be different?

Maybe he'd truly want me.

Maybe I'd let myself have him.

Maybe we could fuck like two normal adults who are attracted to each other.

There is no chance of anything but fucking—not after

the lies and deception. Not after our families made us enemies from the day we were born.

But toe-curling orgasms might make everything more worthwhile. Because Enzo is definitely the kind of man who would ruin me for any man after.

Right now, despite the lust in Enzo's eyes, he won't touch me. His hands are in his pockets as if he's trying to hold himself back with the thin fabric. And the only time he's touched me was to prove a point.

I could want Enzo if I let myself.

If I let go of the pain.

If I let him heal me.

If I forgot all of his wickedness.

If I told him the truth.

But I'm not ready to share what really happened to me yet. If he keeps staring at me though like he's undressing me, then I'll be spilling my guts and stripping my clothes, begging for him to take me.

I'm not ready for that.

But I want to be.

I clear my throat. "So what are we doing about Dallas? We were in charge of his security?" I ask, hoping to put a stop to the sparks flying around the room. We both know nothing is going to happen between us—at least not today. So it's better if we squash all the heat in the room.

Enzo takes his time answering as he pours us both a glass of whiskey. He hands it to me, and I take it but don't plan on drinking much. Last time I drank, I passed out. I'm stronger, but not sure my body is healthy enough to handle any alcohol yet.

He eyes my drink. "Yes, we handle Dallas' security. Most of our clients hire us for security, and we provide it. We also design, build, and sell yachts, but again only to those who want the most secure vessels. And as for what we are going to do about the situation, you should drink some of that first."

"Why?"

"Trust me."

I laugh. "Trust you?"

"Yes."

"Why would I trust you?"

"Because despite what you may think, I do want to do right by you."

I freeze at his words.

"And I want to do what is best for Surrender. You may hate this organization. You may hate the cruelty that happens here, but trust me, we do a lot more protecting the innocent than evil schemes. It just so happens that protecting the innocent involves killing the immoral."

I nod and take a small sip, preparing myself for whatever he's going to say.

"Marry me."

The color drains from my face. "What?"

"Marry me."

He's right; I need more alcohol if we are going to discuss marriage. It's probably buried in that stupid contract somewhere. Or he's going to pull his gun and force me to marry him—although he's never forced me before.

I down my drink. "You must be joking."

"I'm not. We don't have to get married legally. Just go through the motions."

"Why? What would that solve? Are you saying you don't want to go through with the competition? That we will just share the name and power together?"

"No."

"Oh." That would have been nice, ruling with Enzo—

working together. It would have led to endless fights, but the sexual tension would only increase until...

No, don't go there! It's not right.

I turn back to Enzo, his head is cocked, and I can see the vein throbbing on his neck.

Dammit, why do I want him so much?

"We would take pictures of our elopement and pretend to be married. You would go by the name of Black, same as me here. I would say I gave you fifty percent ownership of the company. That way the men would accept your power. And I wouldn't have to explain that I gave up the name of Black and look weak. The company would continue to thrive until we determined the true Black."

"Married," I say the word slowly, trying to absorb it.

"Pretend we are married—that's it."

I sigh. *Be married without any of the perks?*

Except for the power—the money.

Why do they feel like nothing when I wouldn't have Enzo?

Why do I want Enzo?

Fuck.

"And you could do that? Pretend to love me?"

"Easily."

He raises an eyebrow as if asking if I could pretend to love him. *Do lust filled eyes count?* Because I'm afraid that's what I look like right now.

"Wouldn't that make the men think you were a pussy for letting a woman like me have that much power?"

"No, not after they see how strong you are."

Jesus. Why does he have to keep complimenting me? It makes me forget all the shit he did before.

I nod.

"And we won't be legally married?"

"No, no one will ask. And if they do, I'll say we got

married overseas and be able to provide a marriage license that appears real enough. Actually getting married would fuck up the contract between the families, and I don't want that."

"What about Langston and Zeke and—"

"Those close to us will know the truth. But they won't share it with anyone here. Langston, Zeke, Archard, and Westcott will play along because it preserves the empire. We will tell no one else about the contract and fight between us for control of Black."

"What about when the game is over? What then?" I ask.

"Then we get fake divorced and whoever the winner is, stays as Black."

I nod. "You have it all figured out."

"I do."

I don't actually have to go through with a marriage. I just get to use the name Black, same as him and pretend to be his wife while at the club. *Easy enough.* It's the best, for both of us.

"Fine. Let's get fake married."

"Good." Enzo walks over to a painting of a deer on the wall. He slides it open revealing a safe behind it.

I chuckle.

"What?" he asks.

"I just feel like I'm in some sort of spy movie. I didn't realize anyone really kept safes behind paintings."

He shrugs. "This isn't my safe. It belonged to my father, and I haven't opened it since he died."

"Why are you opening it now?"

He enters a code, and it pops open before he reaches inside.

My breathing stops as I wait to see what he's retrieving, but somehow I already know.

A small box appears in his hand. He walks over to me and holds out the box.

I set my glass down on one of the end tables next to several luxury chairs before I carefully take the box from his hands without touching him.

I open the box.

A simple diamond ring sits in the center. I couldn't tell you if it was a princess cut or emerald cut or what. I couldn't tell you if the diamond were real or fake. All I know is it is the most beautiful, elegant ring I've ever seen.

Whoever wore this before wore it with love. I can feel the love oozing from the metal ring.

"It was my mother's," Enzo says.

"It's beautiful."

"If you don't like it, we can get you any ring you want. And when we are done, you can sell it for money. The ring is worth millions. You could live off the money for the rest of your life if you lose."

My gaze slowly drifts up to his—this sad boy's eyes. And in this moment, I forgive him a little more.

For almost killing me.

For forcing me to survive a night in the sea.

For selling me.

For betting against my life and claiming me.

For the lies.

I'm as close as possible to forgiving him for all of it.

Because in his eyes I can see how much this ring means to him. The only treasured possession from a forgotten mother. Something we have in common. A mother who left us and was the only one who ever truly loved us.

Enzo is willing to give it up to provide me with security if I lose.

"You would do that for me?" I ask.

"I don't hate you, Kai. And I abhor what I put you through. Now I just want to protect you. Give you back your life."

I bite my lip as I stare at the ring.

"And I know you don't believe me, but I want to win as much to protect you from this life as to win myself," he says.

I believe him.

I should let him win.

It's what's for the best. But I won't. I want to win. I want to destroy him for the pain he caused me.

"Thank you, but I can only accept the ring for as long as we are fake married. It means too much to you."

"No, you'll keep it."

"I could never sell it."

His eyes darken. "Then I'll sell it for you. This is the only way I can protect you. Take it."

I won't promise him I'll sell it because I won't. Not because I'm not above handouts. Enzo owes me a lot. But I won't use his mother to hurt him.

We are as even as possible—this gesture for his world to see me as his equal and of giving me security afterward.

"Are you going to make me put the ring on myself?" I ask.

His eyes widen at my offer to let him touch me.

He takes the box and removes the ring.

"My heart belongs to the devil," he says reading the inscription on the inside of the ring.

It seems fitting if his mother loved his father.

"You will never get my heart. Nothing more than my captivity I lost in a game, which I will soon win back."

Enzo swallows, and I watch his throat bob. He doesn't agree nor disagree with me.

I hold out my hand, waiting.

43

I push down the anxiety, and then I feel his touch on my hand. My cold interior instantly warms. I feel calm, secure, safe.

Not loved. That's not what this is. We are both too broken to ever experience such a thing.

But it's different—a sense of trust between us, even though we've both lied and will continue to lie to each other.

The lies are to protect each other.

To help each other.

To keep each other safe.

Enzo pushes his mother's ring onto my finger.

And somehow, I think this is the closest I will ever get to being married.

4

ENZO

Married.

It's not real.

It's fake in every way that matters.

But Kai still said yes.

She let me put my mother's ring on her finger.

This is the only "marriage" I will ever have. I will never let a woman into my life; it's too fucking dangerous.

And kids, forget it.

The Black line will end with me.

And if I know Kai, she wouldn't dare bring kids into this world either.

This will end with us.

I stare at the sparkly ring on Kai's finger that fits perfectly, as if it were made for her. I still hold her hand in mine. My thumb lazily playing with the ring on her finger. Waiting for the reaction of fear to surge through her.

It doesn't come.

My heart belongs to the devil. The inscription my mother had inscribed after my father gave her the ring. Good thing Kai's heart is too strong to fall for such a monster like me.

Her big, bold eyes look up at me, as if she can feel my pain through where our hands touch. And I can feel hers.

Too bad this can never be more. I might eventually persuade her into my bed, but that's as far as this will go. When one of us is declared the winner, we will go our separate ways. Then this will be only a terrible memory that we both spend our whole lives trying to forget.

A knock brings us back to reality.

We both take a deep breath in unison. The corner of my mouth twitches with the need to protect her. That's what I do, protect the innocent. And Kai is an innocent. I've failed her before; I won't again.

She smiles softly back trying to reassure me. But this is her first test. This is the first peek at what her life will be like if she wins. And as much as I'd love for her to find a way to win—she's more worthy than I will ever be—the job isn't a kind one, it turns you into the devil. Hardens you until there is nothing left of who you truly are.

It's my burden to bear.

Kai picks up the drink I poured her while I walk over and take a seat in my chair that looks as much like a throne as a chair. I used to hate how my father sat in it, acting like an actual king. But after I've become Black, I understand. The throne has power. And you need every drop of it to control these bastards.

Kai hesitates for a second and then wisely chooses to sit next to me. You don't show that you rise for any man. You sit and let the weasels come to you. You don't show them respect. They are nothing but low life worms that you need to control in order to keep people safe.

Another impatient knock.

"Enter," I say, my voice deep and commanding.

I feel Kai's eyes burn into me. I rarely use my voice like

this in front of her. I know with a single syllable I sound threatening and demeaning—like I could squash everyone in this club with a word. *I could.* That's how powerful my voice is.

The door opens, and Dallas Fell enters.

"You kept me waiting long enough, Black," Dallas spits as he storms in our direction. "I'm tired of your watchdogs holding me back. You fucked up! Now it's time to pay the price!"

I feel Kai shuddering next to me.

You don't belong in this world, this life. Go as soon as you have a chance, I plead. Knowing that even if she heard me, she wouldn't leave. She's too stubborn, bull-headed, and determined. She thinks she can change things, make the world a better place if she were to win. She doesn't understand that I am making the world a better, safer place by handling the criminals myself. No one else can do this job.

"Sit down, Dallas, if you want me to pay for my mistakes," my voice booms, bouncing off the walls in an echo of fierceness.

Dallas scowls but pulls up a chair and sits across from us. His anger is still there, but he seems to accept that I will fix his problems as he eases into the chair.

Until his attention moves to Kai. He must not have seen her when he first entered, but now she's all he can look at.

"Fetch me a drink, whore. And then strip, I want to feast on your body while Black and I do dealings," Dallas says.

Every bead of blood in my body seethes with a furry I haven't felt in years. I feel a tornado of anger and rage swirling, and if Dallas doesn't get out of Surrender, Miami, and the country within the next five minutes, I'll kill him.

Kai just laughs like it was the funniest thing she's heard,

and then she leans forward, playful determination on her face like she's about to tell the sweetest secret.

"Fetch your own fucking drink, jackass. I am not your slave. I won't be doing a damn thing for you. And I sure as hell will never be stripping for anyone but *my husband*." She flashes the diamond I just put on her finger for Dallas to see. Then she places her hand seductively on my inner thigh.

Fuck.

I feel the sweet relief as I always do whenever we touch. The flames flying calm at her touch then start swarming again, but this time in her direction instead of his. *God, I want her so much.*

"Wait? Are you telling me you two—" he starts.

"We eloped last week," I answer.

"Holy shit," Dallas leans back staring between the two of us—accepting her as my wife so easily. I thought I would have to show him our marriage license. Or at least show more affection—kiss her to get him to believe us. Something I'm not sure Kai could handle.

"I suggest you treat my wife with more respect, before I hang you upside down by your balls and leave you writhing in pain for the whole world to see," I say.

"I apologize, Mrs. Black. Please, let us start over. I never meant to treat you with such disrespect. You must be a truly special woman to get a man like Black to settle down and risk everything for you," he says.

She narrows her gaze. "Mr. Black isn't risking anything for me. He loves me, and he knows I am more than capable of living in this dangerous world. I can handle men like you just fine. I accept your apology, for now, but if you say a word against me, the Blacks will no longer work with you in any capacity. You will become our enemy, and it will be you whose life will be threatened."

I grin. *Kickass.*

I couldn't say it better myself.

Dallas smiles as well.

"You have found a fiery match, Mr. Black. I assume you sleep with one eye open to ensure she doesn't cut off your balls in your sleep," he says.

I wink at Kai. "She's everything I ever wanted in a woman. You can see now why I made her my wife to ensure she never became an enemy."

He nods. "Please introduce us properly so we can part as friends."

"Dallas Fell, please let me introduce you to Katherine Black, my wife. Katherine, please meet Dallas, the weasel of the underworld who makes enemies, not just because of how he runs his mouth without thinking, but because he is truly a slimeball who steals from those he claims are his friends. And then expects not to be hunted down like the rat he is," I say.

Dallas chuckles. "That was a good description of me. Thank goodness I have the loyalty of the Blacks to protect me. Pleasure to meet you, my dear," he holds out his hand to Kai.

And for the first time, I see the fear return. The anxiety is apparent in her eyes. She can tolerate touching me and having me touch her for brief moments, but not others. If she shakes his hand, she won't be able to control her fear, and then he'll see her weakness. *He can't see her weakness.* He'd exploit it himself, or sell her weakness to the highest bidder to try and use it against me later.

I can't let them shake hands.

I grab my drink that is filled and thrust it into his

outstretched hand. "We don't have time for any more pleas-antries." I stand and walk over to the bar cart to pour myself a drink before sitting again.

Dallas seems perturbed but sits back and doesn't question why my wife doesn't shake his hand.

"What are your qualms, Dallas? You know the rules. We protect you, but only if you follow our rules. You broke them; we can't protect you if you don't listen," I say.

He chuckles. "So I'm guessing what your lap dog said about there being ten million dollars in my account to replace the lost money is a lie."

My eyes turn devilish. Ten million is nothing to me, but I don't give out money to the undeserving. Of course, it was a lie. I said it to keep him calm while giving Kai and me time to get our stories straight.

"I want to get what I pay for," Dallas says, his eyes heating as he turns to stare at Kai's cleavage.

I growl—low, menacing, and audible.

Dallas doesn't stop. He's testing me. Trying to see if Kai is my weakness. He's that kind of a son of a bitch.

"Beautiful, will you excuse us for a moment? It seems that Dallas needs to be shown some manners," I say. I expect a fight. I expect her to say that she has as much right to be here as I do.

Instead, Kai shoots daggers to Dallas as if he wasn't only looking at her but touching her. Her hate will be what allows her to put away her pride and leave.

This isn't your world, Kai.

This is a world of sick, disgusting men. No woman belongs here. I'm all for equal rights, but there is a reason woman are better than men. They would never let such impure thoughts into their heads.

She stands, peering down at him with disgust. "Hurt my husband, and I'll hurt you. Understand?"

Dallas chuckles in his disgusting way that makes his oversized belly laugh.

"I would never hurt your husband."

She glares. "You did when you took his business and then didn't follow his rules. You put his reputation and mine at risk by letting a breach happen. I may not know everything about this organization or world yet, but I'm a fast learner. I'm not his weakness; I'm his partner. And by being here, I was able to expose your feebleness. That you are a slimy man, who will hit on women giving them no respect. You're lucky I'm letting my husband deal with you instead of dealing with you myself. I'm not as merciful as my husband. And he cares more about money than I do. Because if I dealt with you, you would be wishing you were dead."

Kai storms out swaying her hips and standing taller than I've ever seen her.

This woman.

She says she's not my weakness, but she is. She's my kryptonite. And as soon as she figures it out for herself, I'm a goner.

As soon as the door shuts behind her, I turn back to Dallas.

"Such a firecracker," he says.

"Don't speak about my wife."

He smiles. "Fix your mistake."

"It wasn't my mistake. It was *yours*. And I won't be paying you back. You'll be lucky if I let you leave intact."

He rolls his eyes. "You will because I have leverage now. Your wife is your weak spot."

My heart rumbles in my chest. "Katherine is anything

but a weakness." I struggle to call her Katherine instead of Kai, but it's necessary. No one gets to know she's Kai Miller. It would be too dangerous. I don't know who among us is a snake and who is an ally. Who would take destiny into their own hands and kill her to ensure I win and keep my loyalty.

"We will see."

"No, we won't see. Because you've just sealed your fate. If you think I will let you walk out of here unharmed after threatening my wife, you're deranged."

Color drains from his face.

"I'm sorry, Mr. Black. I didn't mean any disrespect. I've been a long-standing client of your father's and I mistook my place. Your wife is safe. I would never harm her or tell anyone else to harm her. I just meant I can see why you like her so. And I thought it would allow me to get more from our arrangement if I played on your weaknesses. I was wrong. Please show me mercy."

"Why should I?"

"Because I will double your fee. I will pay you more to protect my assets, and I will play by your rules. I value our friendship."

"Ha, we don't have a friendship."

"I value our relationship, and I would never want to become your enemy."

"Fine. You pay double, and I'll let you leave here alive. But if I hear one whisper against my wife, I will hold you personally responsible for the rumors."

He sucks in a breath. "Thank you for your mercy, Mr. Black."

We both stand—our dealings done. I don't keep him alive out of mercy. I keep him alive because he's a weasel that may lead me to who is hunting Kai. I can track him and find out who he's working with easier if he's alive instead of dead.

"Now, help a man out and tell me where you found a woman like Katherine. Who did you buy her from? It's clear from the markings on her body that she was a whore you bought and then marked as your own."

I lose it.

My full furry comes down on him as I punch him in the face. Then riddle him with more punches to every part of his body.

Maybe I was wrong. Maybe he's worth more dead than alive. At least my conscience will survive another day. At least I can protect Kai from one more monster. Because this bastard deserves to die.

5

KAI

I SHUDDER as I storm down the hallway, not able to get away from Dallas fast enough. He's a vile, disgusting man. And as much as I wanted to show my strength, that I'm Enzo's equal, I was happy to have Enzo deal with the wretched man by himself.

Enzo—my fake husband.

I thought we were done with the lies, but at least this time, I'm in on the lie. Everyone else is left seeking the truth.

The ring feels heavy on my finger. The metal frosting against my cold skin as if molding to the temperature of my body.

The ring could ensure my future, even if I lose.

But I won't accept it. I don't need money to survive. To flourish. Not even to live.

I may forever hold hatred and pain for Enzo, but I won't cause Enzo the same pain. I might hurt him, but not by taking the only thing left that reminds him of his mother.

Why would I want any part of this life?

Even if it could provide me with security.

I would lose myself, go mad, if I had to deal with disgusting men like Dallas every day. No wonder Enzo has darkened until there is nothing left but his fiery exterior that is ready to burst every second with a temper that can't be calmed.

I envy the fire in him. It keeps him warm and ensures he never backs down. Never loses himself. Never gives up.

I need to leave.

I need to run.

I need to be free.

I usually wouldn't go back on my word. But after feeling trapped in a room with a man that makes Enzo look like a saint, I have to get to air.

I don't think.

I just go.

My legs moving quickly through the hallways in the shadows. When I pass a group of men, I walk boldly, like I'm their queen.

"Katherine, would you like me to pull the car around for you?" Zeke asks.

I pause realizing he is one of the men in the group. I clench my teeth trying to figure out how to avoid a confrontation.

"Who is the broad?" one of the men asks Zeke.

My eyes tighten into dark holes where only demons can exist as I stare at the group of men. "My name is Katherine Black."

A collective gasp shakes the hallway as every man realizes what it means. One by one they turn their gaze to my hand, searching for the ring I wear.

I purse my lips and stand as proud as possible when they take in my scars trying to determine what they mean.

"I've lived with the devil before I defeated him. And I'll

do the same to any man who crosses me or my husband," I say, knowing I can't show fear or weakness in front of these men. Even though I'm only one woman and they are many. They could hurt me before Enzo ever came to protect me. I have to show my own strength.

I turn to Zeke. "No, Zeke. I won't be needing my car. See that these men return to work."

Zeke eyes me curiously, knowing my claim of Black is a farce. But as Enzo said, Zeke will play along here. Enzo trusts him, so I have no choice but to do the same.

I walk, leaving the men behind to no doubt stare at my ass.

I reach the door that Enzo and I entered the club through. I open the door and let the brightness blind me. I usually seek the dark, but for now, I need the light—something to burn the ickiness from my meeting with Dallas.

"You shouldn't be out here."

The voice sends blood boiling shivers through my body.

"Dad?"

I turn and see my father smoking a cigarette while leaning against the brick wall.

"What are you doing here?" I ask.

He drops the cigarette, putting it out.

"I should ask you the same question."

"You don't get to ask me anything. Not after you've hidden everything from me for my entire life!"

His eyes turn cool. It's where I get my own iciness from —my father.

And suddenly I want to be nothing like him. Because I can't imagine lying to any child of mine for their entire life.

"You don't understand anything, Katherine."

"Then explain to me!"

He shakes his head. "You aren't ready for the truth. You never will be."

"Fucking coward!"

He doesn't flinch as he walks to the door leading into Surrender.

"Wait, you work at Surrender?"

My father doesn't answer, but it's clear from his non-answer that he does.

"You work here. Your whole life is here, yet you never prepared me once for the life I was fated to live in. Enzo's father prepared him his entire life for this life. He prepared him to win. I have no chance. I have nothing because of you!"

My anger overtakes me, and I charge.

"You were supposed to protect me, and you didn't!" I scream as I throw my arm back to punch him.

His hand grabs my fist, stopping me from making contact.

Shooting pain rips through my palm, down my forearm, and into my chest.

My father, a man I should love. The man who raised me. Fed me. Clothed me. Now with his touch wreaks havoc in my body. My body responds like he's the enemy instead of my protector.

Tears water in my eyes, but my father still grips my fist.

"Leave Katherine."

I close my eyes.

Fear, hatred, rage. All of the emotions fill me as my father controls me with his touch. I can't break free.

How can I ever win against Enzo when I can't even tolerate my own father's touch?

I can't.

At least not now—and I don't know how long I have

until the first task, but I will find a way to at least tolerate touch.

I will not be held captive by another man's grasp ever again.

"Let her go," Enzo's voice booms.

My father turns in Enzo's direction, but his grip doesn't loosen.

"I said. Let. Her. Go."

My father lets go, and I can breathe again.

Enzo walks toward us. Each step breathing more life into me with his calm fierceness.

Enzo's eyes run up and down me, looking for any sign that I'm hurt. I'm sure from the expression of terror on my face he thinks my father hurt me.

He did, but not in the way Enzo is imagining. My father hurt me by never protecting me. He was never a real father. True fathers don't lie to their children.

When Enzo is satisfied I'm not truly hurt, he turns back to my father. "Clean up the mess in my office, Miller."

I should cringe at the cruel way Enzo treats my father. But I don't. My father deserves it. And if I can't dish it out, then I'll let Enzo.

My father looks at me one last time. And I see blankness in his eyes. No emotion. No caring. I'm not sure if he ever truly cared about me. Or if I was just the stupid girl who thought her father was different than all the rest.

And as much as I want to feel nothing back, I do. I still feel hope. Hope that the reason my father never told me of this world was for my protection. That he tried to hide me from this world to keep me safe and now that I'm here in it, it hurts him so much that he turned off his emotions.

"Yes, Mr. Rinaldi," my father says, using Enzo's real name.

Enzo frowns, his lips tighten into slits ready to order my father around.

"We aren't done," I say as my father begins to walk inside. My voice has more hope than I wanted to convey. Hope that my father does really love me; he just doesn't know how to protect me now that I'm no longer a child.

My father nods in agreement before disappearing inside to clean up the mess Enzo ordered him to clean up.

Wait...mess?

"What mess is my father cleaning up?"

I stare at Enzo, and that's when I see the cuts on his knuckles. The blood splatter on his jacket.

He killed Dallas.

There is no doubt in my mind.

I can't handle this. Not now.

I turn and start walking away. Where to, I don't know. Just away.

"Wait," Enzo says his hand brushing against the same wrist my father gripped before Enzo realizes what he's doing and begins to pull away.

I place my hand over his, stopping him from letting me go because unlike the pain I felt with my father touched me, I feel something different with Enzo. A feeling I've only ever felt with Enzo. A feeling I can't even describe. I feel weightless, floating through the air above my body. I'm no longer weighed down with grief and anger. I'm flying. I'm free of my past when Enzo touches me.

Every time he does I feel more alive than before. Even when he purposely hurt me with his touch, it wasn't the same as when my father touched me. Enzo's touch calmed me even if it was too much at the same time.

His eyes widen as he looks at us touching.

"I'm sorry. I didn't mean to touch you. You just can't run

off. Our enemies could be lurking nearby. It's not safe to leave without protection," he says.

I barely register his words. All I feel is our bodies connecting in a way that is bigger than the flesh contacting. It's more than emotion or feelings. It's like his presence is bringing me back to life.

I lick my lips.

Why does Enzo's touch save me, when even my own father's hurts me?

6

ENZO

I TOUCH Kai and my world stills.

All of my focus, energy, everything becomes hers.

I've claimed her as mine, but I am just as easily hers. I'm captivated and engrossed in her body. And I would worship at her feet for a chance to be with her.

Despite my desire that grows more restless in my body with each passing second, my lust isn't my focus. My body may be hard and growing harder having her in my clutches. But the calmness on her face covering the pain that was there a moment ago is what has me fascinated.

I shouldn't be able to calm her.

She should tremble every time I touch her. But it seems after I gave her my mother's ring, giving her security for the rest of her life, she no longer feels panic at my touch. By protecting her, I gave up my greatest strength against her. I can no longer control her with a simple caress.

"Does everyone lie to me?" she asks, her hand still holding mine to her wrist in the same place her father was grabbing her when I came out.

Zeke warned me he was concerned Kai would run. He

saw the look in her eyes as she wandered through the hallways.

I knew she needed air after our meeting with Dallas. But I never expected what I saw when I chased after her. I expected her to run as soon as she tasted fresh air. I expected to chase her through the city. Instead, she stood terrified by the grip of her father.

I'd known that he had worked for my father and then me when I took over. As he's a ship captain, I've rarely seen him. He's almost always at sea. But I pay him well as I do all of my men. He shouldn't be living in a trailer. His daughter shouldn't have had to steal to survive. Even if he did owe a debt for his wife's medical bills. He shouldn't have been living with nothing.

And Kai should have had plenty.

Instead, they lived in destitute. Her father lying to her every day about the money he has, who he works for, and even her own destiny.

Seeing him grab her, and the pain it caused her, took every drop of self-control in my body not to attack him. The only thing keeping me from doing so was knowing that he is still Kai's father. That she still loves him despite the pain. And I don't understand his intentions.

My father was the devil. That was clear from the moment I was born. There was no question who he was or what he wanted.

But Kai's father is a mess of contradictions. *Does he love her? Is he trying to protect her by lying? Keep her out of this world? Or is he hiding his demons inside?*

I don't know the answer, but I will find out.

Because if her father is her ally, then I need to keep him away to ensure he doesn't help her win.

And if he is her enemy, then I need to keep him away to protect her.

Either way, Kai needs to stay away from her father.

"Men lie, Kai."

"Why didn't you tell me my father worked for you?"

"The same reason I didn't say that you also worked for me."

"What?"

"When you were cleaning yachts as a teenager you worked for Black."

She pulls her hand from my grasp breaking whatever connection we shared.

"Is the loser required to work for the winner?" she asks.

"No."

Her eyes drop. "Why didn't he tell me the truth? Why didn't he prepare me for this? Why didn't he protect me?"

A tear rolls down her pinked cheek.

I test my newfound theory that my touch can no longer rise panic within her. I stroke her cheek removing the wetness from her face. And the look I get is far more reward than I deserve for such an action.

She bites her lip.

"I don't know why. Only he can answer that."

Her face tightens as she frowns. "And you won't let me speak to him again?"

"No."

"Why?"

"Because I don't trust him."

"Him or me?"

"Him."

She shakes her head. "I don't think you can tell me who I can and can't speak to."

"You're right. I can't, but I'll ensure you never see him so you'll have no chance to speak."

She growls, and her fists fly up and pound into my chest. "You can't keep him from me. He's my father! If I want to talk to him, I will."

I pull her to me, wrapping my arms around her body to keep her from fighting me. But it doesn't stop the wildness in her eyes or the flailing of her body trying to get free in my arms.

"It's for your own good," I say.

"You don't get to determine what's best for me!"

"Yes, I do!"

"No! You sold me! You don't get a say in my life."

"And it's because of my fuck up that I must do everything I can to protect you!"

I let her go.

She takes a step back.

"Keeping me from my father and the truth isn't protecting me."

"It is, and you know it."

She breathes, and I see the fight leave. She knows I'm right. She can't trust her father any more than she can trust me. Her father is trying to protect her by keeping her innocent and weak so she has no chance of winning and becoming part of this life. Or he's a monster who doesn't love his daughter. Maybe there was another sibling that was born. A son he kept hidden trying to raise to take Kai's place, but something happened to that boy, and now it's too late.

My father ordered me to kill Kai when he realized she was my competition. If he knew of a son, he would have done anything to kill the child to ensure I won. My father never thought I was strong enough.

"What if I don't want your protection?"

I take her left hand in mine, my thumb tracing over the diamond sitting on her thin finger. "This ring may not be a vow of marriage. It's not a pledge of my loyalty for all of eternity. It's a vow to protect you, forever. I fucked up once, but now I realize my mistake. I owe you a lifetime of making it up to you, and that means protection, whether you want it or not. I'll protect you with my life."

Another tear falls.

I wipe it away, relishing the chills her skin sends through my body.

"My words aren't meant to make you cry."

She smiles lightly. "To most women, they might sound like heaven, but to me, I realize the truth. Your protection is just another way to control me. I don't want your protection, Enzo."

I sigh as she pulls once again out of my grasp.

"I'm sorry, Kai, but you don't have a choice."

She shakes her head. "I always have a choice. I'd rather die than be controlled."

"I'd rather you be alive."

"Why?"

I shrug. "Maybe saving you from death will absolve me of some of my other sins."

"It won't."

"We'll see."

Kai stares at the door, and I know what she's thinking. Of running inside and finding her father before I banish him. But I'm not the one keeping him from her, he is. He's had every opportunity to speak to her, and yet he's never tried. And I'm going to find out why.

"Come," I say.

It's a command, and I'm not sure she will follow it. As

much as I wish she were truly mine, she's not. She's free willed and does what she wants, even if I know what's best for her.

I smile when I hear her heels on the sidewalk behind me. She catches up with me easily, but then stops in her tracks when she sees where we are headed.

"Go for a ride with me?" I ask as I stare at the gorgeous yacht looming in the distance. If she wants to get over her fear and no longer need my protection; then this is the way to do it—by facing it.

She takes a step back. "No."

How can she survive in this life if she can't face the water?

She can't.

"Then you'll have to accept my offer of protection."

Kai nods silently accepting my words as truth. She doesn't have a choice. If she can't protect herself, then I am all she has.

7

KAI

Enzo wants to protect me.

But it's as much about control as it is protection.

And I'm tired of being a prisoner.

Enzo stops the car outside of his home. *His home*, a place that will never be *mine*. This house will never be anything but my cage. And only I can set myself free.

I throw the car door open and run.

I know it's useless—that Enzo, my captor, will chase. But it feels good to run, to fight, instead, of letting my body fall for the handsome man who offers protection.

That protection can feel good, comforting, safe. But then it also traps me as Enzo can just as easily turn into an insufferable ass who thinks he's God and can control my every movement.

Enzo catches me faster than I expected. We fall to the ground in a lump of arms and legs. I fight. My fists flying into his chest and he lets me.

Pound.

Pound.

Pound.

My fists make contact over and over as I sob into his shoulder.

This is the most contact I've had with him—this exercise in getting out all of my grief.

At first, I continue to take out my pain on him. My frustration and hurt for what he did to cause my current situation overtakes me, allowing me to let it out with my fists in a way I haven't been able to until now. Because now that I can touch him, I'm free of him.

Enzo rolls to his back, and I continue my assault on him. Moving from his chest to his face as I take out my furry. He does nothing but holds my hips as I rest on his.

I punch him until I have nothing left.

And then I collapse on his chest.

I exhale everything inside me, hating him with every breath in my body. Until I hear the thump of his heart, it speeds so fast like he's been running for his life instead of just suffering at the fate of my fists.

Fists that are too weak even to draw blood. He might have a couple of bruises in the morning, but that is the worst that will happen to him. A man like Enzo has faced fists much worse than mine. My assault hardly fazed him, more of a nuisance than real discomfort.

I lift my head, studying him.

"Why is your heart beating so fast?" I ask.

His shifts beneath me, and I feel his hard length between my legs.

"Because you are in my arms."

I gasp.

I've known I turned him on, but I've never felt him. Never felt his desire so plainly displayed for me.

I thought my reaction to realizing the depths of his lust

would be fear. I thought I'd run in terror. Instead, I want to feel more.

I rock, ever so slightly, feeling his erection beneath my body.

"Careful, Kai," Enzo's voice warns as he grits his teeth together as if in pain.

I still. My eyes wide and unyielding.

"Let me go," I say, changing the subject even though our bodies don't agree. I throb, wanting more of him but determined not to give in to the stupid wants of my broken body.

"I can't," he says.

I glare. And I know he will never let me go. Not because his cock is begging for me, but because he thinks of me as his property. He can pretend to be self-righteous all he wants. I know the monster within him.

I get up in a huff, but it feels more like I'm ripping my body from his. Each step I take toward the house is difficult. I want to go back.

What is wrong with me?

I storm into the house.

"Miss Miller, can I get you anything?" Westcott asks as soon as I enter.

"Is Archard here?"

He narrows his gaze. "Yes."

I frown. *Is Archard here to tell me it's time to start the games?*

"Where is he?"

Westcott hesitates. "Mr. Black's office."

I frown at the way he says Enzo's last name, but I won't argue about it now. I stomp to the office.

"I need a word with you, Archard," I say.

He's relaxing on the couch in the office.

"Mr. Rinaldi said you would."

"What? Enzo said I would want to talk to you?"

He nods.

Fuck Enzo.

"And what did he say I wanted to talk to you about?"

"You wanted to speak to Archard about me letting you go," Enzo says from behind me.

I ignore Enzo. "Enzo can't hold me captive. He's no longer Black. He has no power. If this is to be a fair fight, I should be free to leave."

Archard looks over my shoulder to Enzo.

"Don't look at him! Look at me. If you are not loyal to Enzo, then ensure this game is fought fair. I can't properly prepare if I'm a prisoner."

Archard sighs. "You're right. Enzo is no longer Black."

I smile, turning to Enzo to demand he let me go free.

"But there is nothing in the contract between the families that says this game is fought fairly. You are welcome to do whatever acts you please in regards to each other. You can try to undermine, hurt, steal, deter, even kill one another in preparation for the games. The games don't pause just because it's not one of the five tasks."

I gasp.

"Enzo can't use the power of Black to hold you here. But he can use whatever means he desires. Force, wit, lust." Archard stands. "If you want to go free, then you have to figure out how to do it yourself. I can't be involved."

I breathe deeply in and out; my anger is furying inside me.

Archard stops at the door. "I came to let you know preparations have begun for the first game. It won't be too long now."

And then he's gone.

I glare at Enzo. "I will leave."

He shakes his head. "Not until you are safe. You lost fair and square. You're mine until I say you can go."

"There is nothing fair about this."

"No, but that was a lesson you learned long before me."

His eyes glaze over, and I see his cock still straining against his pants.

"You need to shower and change. Your last sin still clings to you," I say talking about the blood on his shirt.

"It wasn't a sin if I was protecting an innocent."

He means me. He thinks he protected my honor or something by killing Dallas.

My eyes focus in on his crotch. I try to imagine what his cock would feel like inside me. *Would it burn my insides as he took me? Or would my body welcome him in, feeling whole for the first time?*

"Don't act like you don't want me," Enzo says, his voice dripping with lust.

"Why haven't you fucked me?" I ask.

"When you ask, I will."

I frown. "What does that mean? It's clear you want me; what's stopping you?"

"I don't hurt women."

"Ha! You don't hurt them yourself; you just sell them and have other men do it for you."

Enzo doesn't argue. And I'm tired of fighting. I need to save all my strength to find a plan to escape and then the rest to pull the truth from my father.

A knock interrupts us.

"Miss Miller, the stylist has arrived," Westcott says.

I exhale, trying to let go of my frustration because I need to get a haircut and new clothes if I want a chance of being taken seriously.

"Thank you, Westcott."

I follow Westcott upstairs to the bedroom I share with Enzo. That will stop. I won't share anything with him—not anymore.

"Claire Holland, this is Mrs. Black," Westcott says, introducing me as Enzo's husband.

I eye Westcott, waiting for him to leave as the perky blond woman approaches me with a broad smile on her face. Westcott leaves us.

"It's a pleasure to meet you, Claire," I say.

She smiles brightly holding her hands out to take mine in hers.

I can't let her touch me.

"I'm so excited to see what clothes you brought." I move past her toward the racks of clothes now hanging throughout the room.

She squeals in delight instead of trying to take my hand again. "I'm so excited to dress you! You have an incredible body, Katherine. So thin! You have to tell me your diet and exercise secrets."

I give her a tight smile. *Get kidnapped and live on a yacht that makes you sick for six years.* "Sure," I say, instead of the truth.

"Westcott said you needed a whole new wardrobe, that you were newly wed and wanted to refresh your clothes?"

"Yes."

"Yay! I'm so excited; we better get started." She moves to the closest rack and starts talking about dresses, when the door opens and Enzo enters.

I glare at him.

"Sorry ladies, I don't mean to intrude. I just need to shower. I won't be in your way. Continue," Enzo says as he strides toward the bathroom.

The bubbly Claire falls silent as she stares wide-eyed at Enzo. Her mouth parts as she drools after my fake husband.

If Enzo notices her gawking, he doesn't give any sign. Instead, he winks at me before disappearing into the bathroom.

I never thought I'd be jealous of any woman staring so openly at Enzo, but I am.

"We should get started," I say, practically hissing between my teeth.

———

I now have enough to fill a large closet with designer clothes. I have a huge pile of makeup and beauty products fit for a queen. Now all that is left is a haircut.

Claire brought with her a large mirror, table, and chair for her to cut my hair. She loves fashion and clothes, but it turns out she started as a hairstylist.

I sit in the chair staring at myself in the mirror as I let my long hair out.

Claire has already been shocked by the scars marking my body. I told her I was in a car accident when I was younger that hurt my body, but I can't hide the long uncut hair. There is no reason for my hair to look like this.

Her mouth falls open as I undo the bun on top of my head and let my ragged, dark hair fall.

"Um...how long has it been since you had a haircut, Katherine?"

"Several years. I got busy and usually wore my hair up, so it didn't matter how uneven it was. But I'd like to get something more modern now."

"Of course," Claire says, smiling. "Let's wash it first, and it will be easier to cut wet."

Enzo still hasn't left the bathroom, even though I heard the shower turn off at least twenty minutes ago.

I walk to the door and slowly open it, peaking my head inside to see Enzo in the closet buttoning up a new dress shirt.

"More business?" I ask as I enter the bathroom.

He shrugs. "You never know when business will arise."

But I realize he isn't dressing in a suit. He's wearing a tux. I remember him saying he wanted to take some photos of us at our fake wedding so we would have some proof if the need arose. He must want to have it happen sooner than later.

Which means once that's done and word spreads that I'm Mrs. Black, it will be even harder to leave the cage I'm in. When Enzo first said he wanted to pretend to be married so we could be seen as equals, I thought he was doing it to help me. Now I think he's doing it to keep me trapped.

"Can I come in?" Claire's high voice rings through the bathroom.

"Yes," I say, not taking my eyes off Enzo's hard chest.

Claire comes in, and I know her eyes are on Enzo the same way mine are.

"Where do you want me?" I ask turning to Claire.

She sighs, and I know the image of Enzo won't soon leave her head.

"Leaning over the tub. That way I can wash your hair and get a feel for your hair's texture," Claire says.

I turn the water on the tub and then kneel before it.

I can do this.

I can do this.

I can do this.

I force my body still as I prepare for Claire to touch me. I close my eyes as I tilt my head forward over the tub, my elbows resting on the tub's edge. My heart races, and my breathing speeds so fast I'm afraid I could have a stroke.

Tears threaten.

Panic rises.

Anxiety overtakes.

I jerk.

And then I feel the touch.

My eyes fly at the warmth. It's too warm to be Claire's hands touching my shoulder. Too warm to be anyone's but Enzo's.

"What are you doing?" I ask as he kneels next to me.

"Washing your hair, and then cutting it," he says.

My eyes search, but I don't see her. "Where is Claire?"

"She's gone."

"Why?"

"Because you had a panic attack. And I won't let you suffer anymore."

I crinkle my nose. I don't remember anything. I don't remember if she touched me or not. I don't remember hearing them talk, but they must have if Claire's gone.

"She laid but a single finger on you before you panicked. You completely locked yourself away into a dark place in your mind. So I sent her away. When I touched you, you came to," Enzo explains.

I frown. I really need a haircut, and I'm frustrated that I can't tolerate anyone touching me for the few minutes it would take to get the job done.

"If she left her scissors, I'll try cutting my hair."

"No, I will."

"Do you know how to cut hair?"

"She gave me a few lessons before she left."

"The water is warm," he says as he tests the water.

He removes the half-buttoned down shirt and then

kneels once again next to me. He waits patiently for me to lean forward. And when I do he gently uses a cup to pour water over my hair.

I close my eyes to keep the water from splashing into my eyes.

"Shampoo," he says, warning me before his hands run through my hair.

I moan at his delicate touch.

His fingers stop, my head tilts, and my eyes open to meet his.

"Sorry," I say, at my unexpected outburst of pleasure.

"Don't be."

He starts scrubbing, his fingers digging into my scalp in the most luxurious, pleasurable way.

I try to keep my moaning inside, but every once in a while, a small whimper escapes through my parted lips.

He stops and rinses my hair before applying conditioner, then rinsing again. His touch on my head warms and sparks every nerve in my body. He could ask anything of me, and I would give it to him, if only he kept scrubbing my head.

"I'm finished," he says almost reluctantly, like he too was enjoying touching my head.

I sit up, and he holds my long strands in his hands before wrapping them in a towel. Then he leads me to a chair he set up in the bathroom in front of the mirror. He removes the towel and watches my wet hair fall.

He picks up scissors lying on the counter.

"Um.." He clears his ruff throat. "How short do you want it?"

I motion to just above my breasts indicating where I want him to cut.

He nods and swallows, his Adam's apple bobs as he does.

He pulls my hair back gently.

"You trust me?" he asks with a grin.

I nod silently. Because I do trust him—*too much.*

It gives him too much power over me.

I watch his breath rise and fall in his chest slowly as he takes my strands in his hands and begins to work. I feel my head getting lighter with each snip. I enjoy watching the focused look of his brow as he works. His concentration stays on my hair and not me—giving me a chance to study him. The scars on his chest. The muscles that seem to grow bigger with each passing day.

My mouth waters thinking of what it would feel like to kiss his abs. Slip my tongue between the hard ripples. Feel his muscular body between my legs. I feel my body heat and not just from Enzo's warm touch. For a desire to have him.

"Finished. What do you think?"

I flick my hair in front and watch the even strands fall to the length I asked Enzo to cut it.

"I'm impressed. When you lose your empire to me, you should take up hair styling," I tease.

He smiles. "If it means I get to cut your hair, then I'll do it."

I give him a weak smile. *How can he be so kind to me?*

He's a monster. He hurt me. This is just an act.

But it's what makes me fall for him. It's what tricks my mind and allows my body to take over which is desperate to feel him—to fuck him.

Enzo is attracted to me too, but not enough to act on it. And I will never show weakness by asking for the man who sold me to fuck me. No matter how much I want his body. No matter if it would heal me to feel that of a man who I actually desire inside me. I will not give him the satisfaction of knowing I want him.

And Enzo isn't attracted enough to me to actually woo me—no man is.

So I'm destined to live out the rest of my years alone.

Enzo steps back. "There is a white dress I picked for you to wear hanging in the closet. Put it on, and then Westcott will take some pictures he can send to the newspapers."

And just like that Enzo is back to ordering me around. He leaves before I go in search of the dress that will serve as my fake wedding dress. I open the closet door and see the most beautiful lace dress.

Can a monster really pick out something so beautiful? Can the devil protect an angel?

Not without clipping her wings.

8

ENZO

I PREPARE for Kai to yell at me for my plan. She's not going to like the location of our fake wedding.

I stand at the base of the stairs in my tuxedo. I considered wearing something more casual, but I need this to look as convincing as possible.

Kai's feet clink loudly on the stairs as she descends. And I try to keep my eyes down. I know my body will betray me when I look at her and show how desperately I want her. I can't imagine her looking like anything except a beautiful angel in her dress. A dress I'll want to rip from her flesh as I drive my cock inside her. And I need as much self-control as possible to keep my hands off her after getting the pleasure of feeling her silky hair in my hands.

But after two steps, I can't help but look.

Gorgeous doesn't do her justice. The lace dress clings to her body, giving her curves I didn't realize she had. She's curled her hair, and it hangs elegantly to just above her chest. She's painted her face with a light layer of makeup that highlights more than overpowers her features. But her dress is anything but angelic. It's sexy as fuck. There is a slit up to her thigh I didn't realize existed when I picked the dress from Claire's cart of clothes and the V at the top dips down to between her breasts. The dress is as fit for a red carpet as it is for a wedding, but it will do perfectly for the pictures.

I just have to persuade my cock to behave.

"How do I look?" she asks when she hits the last step.

I smirk. "You already know from the heat in my eyes."

She smiles. "You don't get to touch me," she warns.

"I get to touch you plenty. We are supposed to act like we are married."

Her cheeks flush.

I hold out my hand, and to my surprise she takes it. Maybe this will be less of a fight than I thought.

"Are we back on good terms? Or are you going to try to run again?"

"You cut my hair. I guess I owe you."

I lead her to the back door. "Good, because it's going to take all of your strength to repay me."

I can see from her amused expression she thinks I'm asking for sex, until I nod in the direction I'm leading her where an arch of flowers hangs in front of the ocean.

"You're kidding. I can't go there."

"Where else do you suggest our fake wedding take place?"

She sighs. "Fine, but I'm only giving you five minutes. And my face will be wrinkled with anxiety the whole time. I'm not exactly sure those will be the pictures that will convince the world we are married."

I grin. "Trust me." Because I already know this is more than just about getting some wedding pictures. This is about getting Kai one step closer to being free.

I lead her out of the house onto the back deck. She goes easily; the harder part will be when we reach the sand.

"Ready?" I ask.

Her eyes grow large. "Don't let me go," she whispers, gripping my hand tighter.

I don't plan to. *Ever*.

In unison, we step down from the last step onto the corse sand. Kai isn't wearing any shoes, and she wrinkles her nose as the warmth tickles the bottom of her foot.

I don't take my eyes off her face. She doesn't react in anxiety. But then it's not the sand that she fears. It's the water. The sea. The danger.

I hear Westcott move to the deck behind us, ready to take pictures of us as we walk hand in hand to our fake wedding.

"You got this," I say as we take another step.

"I don't need a pep talk."

I smile, Kai's sassy as always.

Another step, and then another, inches us closer. With each step, I wait for the panic and anxiety to rise in her. Instead, I feel her squeeze my hand tighter.

"Who's that?" she asks.

I look in the direction her eyes travel to the man walking to the arch.

"Our fake priest."

She smiles. "This is crazy."

"Don't worry; soon we will be getting fake divorced."

This earns me a tiny laugh. Something I rarely see and want more of. But doubt I will see it again. I don't deserve it. And our future together will be riddled with more pain.

The arch of flowers sits several feet from the edge of the ocean. And we make it all the way without a panic attack.

"Maybe you've been cured," I say.

She shakes her head. "No, this is just far enough away that the water doesn't scare me."

I take her other hand, and we face each other standing in front of our fake priest. Maybe it's my touch and presence that calms her.

I reach up and pluck a red flower from the arch, before tucking it behind her ear.

Her cheeks blush, and her eyes brighten in a thank you.

"What are we supposed to do now? I've never been to a wedding," she says.

"Me neither."

Justin leans in. "Just stand here and promise each other the world even though you will likely cheat and lie within the first month of marriage resulting in one or both of you having your heart ripped out."

We both raise an eyebrow at our fake minister.

"Sorry, I didn't mean to interrupt. I'm Justin."

"Kai—"

"Katherine, this is my wife, Katherine. And I'm Enzo."

Kai stares at me, at my correction of her name. I hired him under the guise that we wanted to relive our marriage in photos since we eloped and didn't hire a photographer the first time.

"I'm sure you two will beat the odds and live a long and happy life together."

Kai laughs. "I'm sure we will."

Justin smiles. "Would you two like a private moment to relive the vows you said to each other before?"

"No, we remember our vows just fine."

He smiles.

Kai's eyes cut to Westcott who has been firing off photos of us from the deck. He's not a professional photographer, but I figure the fewer people we could involve in this the better. Especially since I haven't decided if I want to announce our marriage or not. Not after how Dallas reacted. I don't know if it will help to pretend we are married. It doesn't hurt to have options though.

A wave crashes next to us, spitting drops of water onto our skin.

Kai tenses and tries to pull away, but I hold her hands firmer in mine.

"You two make a cute couple," Justin says.

"Thanks. I think we got all the pictures we need. You are welcome to go."

Justin frowns shaking his head. "I think you are forgetting one important picture."

Kai and I both turn to him with a raised eyebrow.

"What?" Kai asks.

"You got a picture of you walking together, holding each other, pretending to say your vows. I'm sure you'll get pictures of the ring you gave her. But none of that matters without the kiss."

Kiss.

"I don't think that's necessary," I say. "We remember our first kiss without a picture to remind us." These pictures are just to prove that we were married. Something I can show to people, display in my office, put online as proof.

Kai turns back to me trembling slightly. "Kiss me."

"What?"

"Kiss me, my husband."

I don't care that Justin is still watching us, I let the shock read all over my face.

Why does she want me to kiss her?

We have had an attraction to each other since the moment I met her in the bar. And it came back as quickly when she came back to me in Surrender, after spending years apart.

But she hates me—I want her to hate me. Because as much as I want her, I don't deserve her.

It's just a kiss. I've kissed her before. It's innocent enough. It's her motives I don't understand. *Why does she want me to kiss her?*

"Enzo."

I freeze.

I can't.

She can see it on my face—which for some reason makes her light up more.

"Thank you, Justin," she says.

He nods to us both. "Best of luck."

He heads back up the beach.

"Ready to head back?" I ask.

She laughs. "No."

I cock my head.

And then she jerks my hands toward her as our bodies collide and our lips crash together.

This kiss isn't clumsy or innocent. Not like the kisses I stole from her when we were teenagers. This kiss clutches at my heart begging me to finally feel something for this woman beyond regret, pain, and anger.

Her tongue parts my lips, and I know I won't be able to stop, not now that I've had her.

I grab her hips forcefully with a promise never to let her go. Her arms wrap around my neck as I take over the kiss, strengthening it with my own fire. My tongue pushes deep inside her mouth begging her to open wider for me. To let me in. To take this further.

She moans against my lips. Welcoming me in through

her shields of ice. I've never felt such a strong desire for a woman before.

"Jesus, Kai."

She runs her tongue over her bottom lip before I pull it back into my mouth. Sucking, tasting, enjoying. I explore every inch of her mouth as my self-control evaporates.

My hands need to be everywhere. And I let them roam her body without thinking.

Down her back in the backless dress.

Over the lace fabric covering her glorious ass.

Up her sharp hips, to her tiny waist—to her cleavage.

I don't think.

I squeeze her breasts. *God, I've wanted to feel her body again for weeks now.* And hearing the tiny whimpers in her throat as I massage her breasts drive me wild.

I sweep her long hair off her neck and kiss her exposed skin that's like ice to my lips. I love how our differences in temperature only heighten the experience. I forgot how incredible it feels. Like tiny explosions firing every time I touch her.

I grab the hem of her dress hiking it up her body as I feel every part of her thigh. The rough scars ripple under my fingers where smooth skin should be.

Fuck.

What am I doing?

I have to stop.

But I don't.

It's like she's possessing me. It would take a nuclear explosion to stop me, and even then, I'm not sure I would stop until I was dead.

This is what makes Kai dangerous to me. This control she has. I've always prided myself on my self-control, but with Kai, it's different. She's different than all of the rest of the girls I've been with. She could consume me whole if I let her.

Stop.

My hand slides higher to her ass. *Jesus, she's not wearing any underwear.*

Stop.

I open my eyes, hoping a pained expression on her face will persuade me to release her before things go too far and I make the hatred she feels for me permanent. Not that that would necessarily be a bad thing. Her hating me might make protecting her easier.

When I open my eyes though, I don't see pain on her face. Nor terror, anxiety, or fear.

Kai's lost in the moment, sucking it all up, and begging for more with her lips as her body presses deeper into me.

Beautiful.

There is no reason to stop—she wants this.

I press into her, my cock pushing against her stomach when I really want it pressing much lower and deeper into her. So that's what I do.

I lift her up, and her legs wrap around me. My cock driving against her pussy as her legs tighten around me, trying to suffocate me like a boa constricting its prey.

Stop.

I kiss down her neck, to the curve of her upper breast. *More, I need more.*

I nudge the fabric of her dress off her breast, exposing it to the world. Good thing this is a private beach because I would gorge out anyone's eyes who saw her glorious breasts.

She gasps as my mouth envelopes her nipple pointed at me, begging for me to tease and taunt.

More, more, more.

Stop.

The voices continue taunting me—wanting one thing and knowing I should do the other. Like the devil and angel on my shoulder. But the devil will always win, because I was born from the devil. There is too much of my father in me. He still has a hold over me, even in death.

I'm not strong enough to stop this—not until some force of power greater than me ends this.

The water.

I just have to force my legs to the water.

Kai grabs my neck, sinking her nails into my nape as she plants a passionate kiss on my lips.

Fuck, she isn't going to make this easy.

I get lost in the kiss, forgetting my mission until a wave splashes against my feet. The tide is rising, getting closer, meeting me halfway.

I hold onto Kai tightly and begin walking. I expect her to panic as soon as she realizes where I'm headed.

She doesn't.

She's too consumed with our kiss. Too lost. Too desperate.

She begins undoing my tie, loosening it while her legs grip me tighter.

My legs move automatically toward the water allowing me to deepen our kisses, while pulling at her dress, practically ripping pieces from her body.

Kai is everything.

If only this were possible.

I feel the water on my feet covering to my ankles, and I want to run in the other direction because I know how this will end. Instead, I take another step until the water is to my knees.

Kai still doesn't recognize what's happening. Her eyes

are closed, and her body so lost in mine that fireworks could go off and I don't think she'd notice beyond the sparks flying between us.

End this.

Run.

I don't have the strength to stop this. All I have left is to fall.

The water engulfs us, and our bodies fly apart as if the waves forced us apart.

When I break the surface, Kai is flailing in the water.

"You fucking asshole!" she screams as she makes it to her feet, pulling her soaked dress up to cover her body.

The spell I was under breaks instantly at the loss of our connection.

I can't touch her—nothing beyond the most chaste of touches ever again. Our connection is too much for my self-control.

I'm just like my father.

Worse.

Because I pretend I only hurt the wicked, when in fact I am just as capable of hurting the beautiful—just like my father did.

Kai runs out of the water. And I chase after.

"Kai, stop!"

She does finally stop on the edge of the deck, whipping around with a cross look on her face.

"Why should I? You are a fucking bastard! You know how much I'm afraid of the water. Why would you do that?"

I stiffen. "Because I want to ruin you," I lie. *Because it's the only way to save you from me.*

She gives me a sly smile. "Don't worry; I'll ruin you first."

She stomps toward the house, and I follow. She throws

open the sliding door and steps inside, walking through my house not caring that she's getting water all over my hardwood floor.

I follow.

We both head upstairs to the bathroom.

Kai begins stripping out of her dress when she stops, noticing that I followed her.

"You've got to be kidding? Do you really think I'm going to let you watch me strip after what you did?" she says.

"I'm dripping wet. I'm going to shower and change."

"You're not going to do that here."

"This is my house and my bathroom," I growl.

She smirks. "Not anymore. Get out!"

I roll my eyes but decide not to fight her on this. I walk into the closet to grab a pair of jeans and a T-shirt and storm out to go shower in the guest bathroom. Too bad cold showers don't work on me anymore because of Kai. I'm going to need something to convince my aching balls nothing is ever going to happen with her.

Twenty-minutes later I'm still steaming, but a knock on the door changes things.

"Come to apologize for kicking me out?" I ask as I open the door.

"We need to head out right now. The Savage sent out a mayday," Zeke.

"Shit."

I throw my shirt on as I race after Zeke. The Savage is the head of our fleet. It's the yacht I'm most often on. My favorite. Anders captains the ship for me. He's the best captain in my crew. If he sent out a mayday, then they were attacked by the best.

"Do we know what happened yet?"

"No, they've been radio silent ever since."

"Shit." Which means we were definitely attacked.

"Where's Kai?" Zeke asks.

"Probably still showering."

Zeke stops abruptly. "You need to get her."

"Why?"

"Because now that you are no longer Black, she has to come with us. Archard is downstairs. He heard the mayday call. You can't make this decision by yourself."

"Kai get your ass downstairs in the next five-seconds! Archard has something he needs to say," I holler, pretending Archard is here to tell us the game starts tomorrow. Instead of the truth.

The bedroom door flies open, and Kai emerges in tiny shorts and an oversized shirt of mine.

"Is the game starting?" she asks with a hint of trepidation in her eyes.

I ignore her and head downstairs.

She follows.

"Archard, is the game starting?" Kai asks.

Archard shakes his head. "No, I'm just here to ensure the rules are followed."

Kai looks to me then Zeke.

"We need to go," I say.

"Go where?" she asks.

"The docks. We need to get on a yacht right away. The Savage, one of our main vessels, sent out a mayday. We think we've been attacked," I say.

"Why are we going to the docks? How will that help?" Kai asks.

"We need to get on a boat and hunt down the bastards who attacked us."

"We?"

"Yes, *we*. We will lead a crew of men. I don't leave my

men to take care of things themselves, not when it's this important."

"I can't get on a boat."

I narrow my gaze. "You're going to have to."

"No, I don't." Kai crosses her arms and stares at Archard, knowing she has his reassurance to back up her words.

I run my hand through my hair in frustration.

"We have to go! We don't have a choice. I don't leave my men when they need me."

"You no longer get to make the decision yourself."

"Goddammit, woman! You are the most infuriating person on the planet!"

"And you are the most selfish, demeaning asshole!"

"What the fuck do we do, Archard?"

"You don't both have to go, you just both have to agree how to handle the situation as a leader, or you don't get to be involved at all," he answers.

"Fine, I'll go. You stay." I like that plan better anyway. I have a feeling this is Alastar's men who attacked us. This sounds like his doing. He is my biggest rival. He's wanted my money and power for a long time. And I don't know if Alastar was the leader Jarod reported to. If his men are hunting us and want Kai back, I don't want her anywhere near them. *She's mine.*

"Like hell I'm letting you go! You'll get to make whatever fucking decisions you want by yourself if you go. The men will continue to see you as the leader instead of seeing me as an equal. You can't go."

"Jesus Christ! All I'll do is ensure my men are safe."

"Our men." Blood boils raging back and forth between us.

"I'm going."

"No, you're not."

ELLA MILES

I narrow my eyes as my cheeks redden, and my teeth grit to hold back my anger. I walk to her so I can hiss in her ear. "You are just doing this to get back at me."

Her eyes cut to mine. "You hurt me; I hurt you."

"You have no idea what you are doing."

"I'm ensuring you have the same power as me. I'm punishing you for hurting me because you can't stand not to have all the control."

"I won't leave my men to die."

"We will send Zeke and Langston," she says.

Zeke looks at me. We've already wasted too much time as it is. "Go." Hopefully, I'll be able to coerce Kai into letting me follow suit.

"And keep us informed of what is happening," Kai says.

I chuckle. She has no idea what we are facing. Zeke won't be able to give us a play by play. We won't know what happens until he returns.

"Stay safe," I say.

"Always do," Zeke answers and then disappears.

"Fuck!" I scream before pounding my fist into the wall leaving a large hole in its wake. I've never stayed behind when something this bad happened before. I hate not being there for my men.

"It's going to be fine. Not everyone needs an ass like you weighing them down."

"Oh sweetie, you have no idea the danger you've just put our entire team in, and yourself, by not letting me go after them. My men are fearless, but they need a leader. Zeke and Langston aren't those men. We always fight together—the three of us. If anything happens to any of them, it's on you. And when the danger isn't put out, you'll be who they come for next."

"Where are you going?" she asks as I storm toward the office.

"To work and hope I can find some way to help them from here." But I already know there is nothing to be done. Kai may try to seek further revenge, but I can't imagine anything worse than this. Whatever Kai plans after this will be nothing. At least I no longer have to worry about any physical connection between us, she just severed it.

9

KAI

Fuck, that kiss.

That kiss was everything.

Passionate.

Gut-turning.

Toe-curling.

Explosions firing.

I never wanted the kiss to end. I was completely lost in the moment. I forgot about everything.

The pain.

The heartache.

The game.

Everything.

I forgot it all.

Nothing has ever consumed me as much as kissing Enzo did—until he dumped us in the water.

And then the hatred returned, more powerful than ever. Like I was baptized in the water and came up new. The lust vanished, replaced fully with the hate—and the need to destroy this man that has been the cause of every bad thing in my life.

Enzo is a monster. Not just to men who deserve it. He's the devil through and through. I never met his father, but Enzo is just like him if his father is as bad as everyone says.

And the best way to destroy a monster is to show them their reflection. Once Enzo sees his reflection as the devil he truly is, he will destroy himself. He won't be able to live with the self-loathing when I'm through revealing his truths.

I pound on the door Enzo threw shut to his office.

"Let me in!"

"No."

"You don't have a choice! I get to be involved in the business."

"What? You going to run to Archard if I don't let you in?"

"If I have to."

Archard left shortly after Zeke did, but not before warning us both that not following the rules would lead to penalties during the game.

I hear the lock of the door clink, and then the door opens. Enzo stands tall, towering over me. The look alone would bring most men to their knees, but I know Enzo's weakness—*me*.

"I'm sorry," I say.

He huffs. "No, you're not."

Enzo collapses into the office chair, while I take a seat on the couch.

"Fine, I'm not. But I didn't make the decision to get back at you from before."

"Then why did you?"

I hesitate. "Because I couldn't go with you, and I don't trust you." *And I would be petrified, worrying they might hurt you. I want to be the one who hurts you.* My feelings are so messed up.

He cracks his neck.

"What are we going to do now?" I ask.

"Nothing. There is nothing to do but wait. Zeke will call when he has the situation under control."

"Who attacked us?'

"I think Alastar. He's been trying to coordinate his allies to make a move against us for a long time. I've been distracted lately. They must have known and made a move."

"How dangerous is he?"

"A step below me."

"So basically an adorable, whiny kitten."

"This isn't a joke, Kai."

"Sorry, just trying to lighten the mood."

A knock rattles. "Excuse me, sir. I have the pictures on my camera here. You wanted one selected to send to the newspaper for the announcement. Would you like to choose?"

"Leave the camera on my desk," Enzo says.

Westcott places the camera on his desk and then leaves.

We both stare at it, silently stewing until I can't take it anymore.

I retrieve the camera, and kick my legs up on the couch, while I click through the pictures.

There are hundreds of pictures. Of us holding hands as we walk through the sand. Then staring at each other. Some of us smiling and laughing. Others more solemn.

I smile looking at us. We look like a bride and groom on our wedding day.

And then I get to the picture of us kissing. How locked in the moment we are. How right we look together—like we belong in each other's arms.

It was so easy to kiss him. To let him hold me, like we regularly make out while holding each other.

"Why the hell do I let you touch me like this when I can't even shake anyone else's hands?" I say.

"Because we have a physical connection neither of us can shake," Enzo says standing over me as he stares down at the picture of us making out. "And it's going to cause the death of both of us if we aren't careful."

He lifts my legs and then sits on the couch before placing my feet in his lap.

This feels so normal, how any regular couple might sit on this couch. Except one of us didn't try to kill the other. One of us didn't sell the other. One of us is cruel. And the other is about to get her revenge by ruining him and then winning this fucking game.

I reach out and touch his hand, trying to unnerve him, but instead, I do it to myself. I feel everything he's feeling when I touch him: the worry, fear, and concern for his friends.

Shit, what did I do?

I'm not a monster. I shouldn't stoop to his level. And I sure as hell shouldn't bring other people's lives into this.

"I'm sorry—truly."

I continue tracing circles on his palms, each circle I trace I feel more of his emotions. More pain. More hurt. More anger.

But also lust, desire, want.

He grabs my wrist and lifts my fingers from his palm. "Stop."

"Why?"

"Because if you don't, I won't be able to."

And what if I don't want you to stop? Enzo is the only one who has been able to drive out my demons so far. If we fuck, maybe they will be gone for good.

Enzo sighs. "Try to sleep, Kai. It's going to be a long night." He leans his head back and closes his eyes.

I swear I hear him snoring a few minutes later. Apparently, sleeping is how he shuts the world out when he wants to.

I close my eyes, but I know I won't be able to sleep. Not on this tiny couch with my legs on Enzo. Not with the tension between us. Not when I want him more than I want any sort of revenge.

Christ, what's wrong with me? How can I lust after a man who hurt me so much?

Because there are two sides to Enzo. The monster and the protector. Turns out I like it when he protects me. Because him staying home instead of going to the fight feels like protection. If he truly wanted to go, he would have fought harder.

I try to push Enzo out while I wait for news, but hours pass, and he's still the only thing on my mind. And I'm more conflicted than I've ever been about what I want and what I plan on doing next.

"Enzo!" Langston yells down the hallway.

Enzo's eyes pop open, and we both run at toward Langston's distant voice.

The front door is open, and Langston stands inside, holding a limp and bleeding Zeke in his arms.

Fuck. I fucked up.

10

ENZO

If Zeke dies, I'll kill her.

I don't care that I've done everything I can to keep Kai alive. I don't care if she's too naive to realize the danger she put us all in. I don't care if she genuinely thought she was doing the right thing.

She's no longer innocent.

She fucked up.

She betrayed me. She betrayed Zeke. She betrayed all of my men.

I run to Langston. "What happened?"

"We were ambushed. It was all a setup, a trap. They used the attack on The Savage as bait. They wanted you, Enzo."

"How many did we lose?"

Langston's eyes drop. "We were the only ones to get out. And it wasn't because I was skilled. They let us go. They wanted us to go—to warn you."

Fuck. My enemies already think I'm weak. I need to squash them immediately—set an example.

"There are rumors you no longer are king. That you've abandoned your thrown—for pussy." Langston looks to Kai.

I don't have time to deal with it now. Now I need to ensure Zeke lives.

"Put him on the couch," I yell to Langston.

He does. There is so much blood. I've seen bad before, but I'm not sure I've seen a man continue to breathe with this much blood loss.

I stare at Kai who blinks rapidly as she takes in the scene. I toss her my cell phone from my pocket. "Call the emergency doctor listed in my contacts. Now!"

She starts fumbling with the phone.

I don't have time to ensure she does it. I need to take care of Zeke.

"Hang on, buddy. You're going to be fine. I got you," I say, but Zeke doesn't stir. He doesn't even open his eyes or moan.

I rip his shirt open, trying to identify his wounds to stop the bleeding.

Three holes cover his chest.

Fuck.

Langston and I exchange a quick, worried glance. He has less than a five percent chance of surviving and that's being generous.

"The first aid kit!" I yell to Langston who is already moving to where I keep it in the cabinet on the wall for emergencies just like this.

He opens the box and starts pulling out all the gauze he can find. I find the first bullet wound on his stomach spurting the most blood and pack the gauze tightly over the wound.

Langston does the same for the two wounds on his upper chest.

"Just hang on, Zeke," I repeat.

I scan more of his body trying to find other sources of the bleeding.

His jeans are soaked in red blood.

And then I see the slice on his upper thigh less than an inch from his groin.

Jesus, these men are savages. They tried to castrate my most loyal man. They won't get away with this.

"I need more gauze," I shout to Langston.

Langston's eyes grow big. "There's none left."

"Fuck!"

I stare down at what we have, but if I remove any of the already soaked gauze from his current wounds, he'll die. But if I don't stop the bleeding in his thigh, he'll die. Whatever I do, he'll die.

"Here," Kai says, pulling her shirt from her body and tossing it on his leg.

I cover the wound with the shirt, pressing hard and deep.

"Let me," she says, kneeling next to me.

I want to push her away and say she has no right to touch him, not when she is the reason he will die. If I had been there, this would have never happened. I have instincts my father taught me that Langston and Zeke don't. I would have realized the trap that was set.

"Push down hard on the wound with everything you have. Use your entire body," I say.

She nods, her fingers brushing against mine as she takes over applying pressure on his leg. When our fingers touch, I no longer feel the spark of connection. Instead, I feel anger and hatred. I've never wanted to punish someone so much in my life.

Never.

Kai has no idea what Zeke means to me, what Langston means. They are truly my family. Two of only a handful of people who actually care if I live or die—and she put a member of my family at risk.

Unacceptable.

She's not cut out for this life. And the sooner she realizes it, the sooner I can take over as Black again, on my own.

Langston goes white staring at Zeke.

"Is he breathing?" I ask.

"No."

"Don't you dare die on me!" I yell, my voice cracking as I scream. I don't get emotional often. I haven't cried since I was a kid, but I feel the water clouding my eyes. My heart aches and pounds in my chest. "Trade with me," I say to Langston.

He nods and moves, too shaken up to think straight.

I put my lips over Zeke's, breathing life into him, while applying pressure to his chest wounds. Langton struggles to contain the blood spurting from Zeke's stomach.

His chest rises and falls, confirming that oxygen is getting in, but I know his heart isn't beating hard enough to push what little blood is left in his body through his veins.

I start pumping over his heart, demanding it beat faster.

"You don't get to die, Zeke! Not today! Do you hear me?! You don't get to fucking die," I scream, as I continue to pump my hands over his heart, while Langston and Kai do their best to keep the blood inside his body.

I hear footsteps down the hallway. Westcott opens the front door to let the doctor in.

Finally.

I look to Langston and Kai who have yet to notice that help is on the way. The sound is too faint for either of them to hear or notice. But the doctor is coming.

I can't save Zeke, I'm not strong enough, but I have enough money and resources to pay for the best team. If anyone can save him, they can.

Footsteps grow louder as they run down the hallway to where we lay.

The door crashes open and a team of six doctors and nurses race inside, the lead doctor, Lester Patten, is in the front.

Thank fuck I pay him well enough to drop everything and come, no questions asked.

This isn't the first time he's had to come to save one of my men or me, but this is the worst he's ever had to deal with.

Patten's face falls ashen for a second when he makes a quick visual assessment of the situation. And my fears are confirmed—this is bad.

"Get him on the gurney. Now. We need to perform a surgery," Patten says.

The team descends, taking all of our places as they cover the wounds and move Zeke to a gurney.

"He's not breathing," I say, my voice suddenly calmer now that I've accepted that Zeke will most likely die and there is nothing left for me to do here.

Patten looks to one of his men, who immediately starts performing CPR, while the rest pack in his wounds with more gauze to try and stop the bleeding.

"You should find everything you need to perform surgery in the room down the hall," I say, even though the doctor and his team already know which room to head to. I have one room that is always set up for this exact situation. You can never be too careful. We don't have time to get to the hospital. And even if we made it, Zeke wouldn't be safe there. Alastar's men would try to kill one of us there.

"I know," Patten says.

And then they are gone—whizzing Zeke down the hallway to do what I paid for—everything fucking possible to save his life.

Langston looks at me a second, trying to be loyal to me, but needing to go watch over Zeke. His eyes are red with worry, his cheeks stained with tears that must have fallen at some point, his face still white from shock, and his body tense with fear.

"Go," I say.

He doesn't wait for a second order. He leaves.

"I'm so sorry, Enzo," Kai says.

I close my eyes trying to conjure all the self-control I can muster. But Zeke's blood still clings to my fingers and clothes. I can't let what happened go.

"Do you have any idea what you just did?!" I scream at Kai.

Her lip trembles as my voice beams through the room, ricocheting off walls and pouring into her as if I just used my fists instead of my voice.

"I didn't realize—"

"Exactly. You don't fucking belong in this world. You have no idea what it takes to be Black. If you were to win, all you would do is get yourself and my entire organization killed. Your first decision as Black got Zeke killed!"

"He's not dead—"

"He might as well be."

"The doctor can save him."

My eyes protrude with all of my furry. My fists ball, my nostrils flare, and my heart pounds so loud I'm sure she can hear it.

"If he lives, he will carry scars with him forever. You of all people should know that."

A slow tear rolls down her cheek.

"You don't get to cry. You don't get to feel sorry for what you did. You may not have killed anyone before, but you just did—you killed Zeke."

More tears fall down her cheek, but I harden more. *I will destroy her.* I don't know why part of me felt any amount of sorrow for her before, but it's gone. I want Archard to walk in the door now and say the game starts tomorrow, because I need to take out my frustration on her, now. And killing her wouldn't be enough.

I need to find a way to fix this. Since I won't kill Kai, and I want her alive and healthy when I do my damage to her, I have to take my rage out in a different way. By ensuring everyone fucking knows I'm Black, and I don't show mercy. Alastar's men will die a torturous death for what they did to Zeke.

And then everyone will know why Kai is married to me. They will know I won her. And marrying her was just a way to claim her as mine. I'll make her nothing.

I start toward the door. "I'm leaving."

"What? Where are you going?" Kai asks.

"To get revenge for Zeke."

"But Zeke needs you here, if he wakes up—"

"Langston will be here if he wakes up." *Which is a big if.* "And when he wakes up, I want to be able to tell him I killed the man who hurt him. We can't show weakness, not fucking now."

"But—" Kai puts her hand on me.

I jerk back, like her touch burns me—I hate her.

I see the pain from my reaction on her face. "Don't you dare try to stop me! You stopped me from going before, and Zeke paid the price. If you try to stop me now, I'll kill you."

She doesn't terror at my threat. She stands tall, strong, fearless.

Fuck her.

"And I would deserve it."

I narrow my eyes. Not believing she said that. But nothing she says will fix anything—*nothing*.

"Go."

"I don't need your fucking permission."

"And I'm not giving it."

I shudder as my anger fills me, needing a fucking escape hatch through my body. And then I disappear.

Without Kai's permission.

Without Archard holding me back.

I go because it's the only thing I can do for Zeke. A man who saved me too many times to count. My brother in every way that matters.

I failed him. I won't fail him again. I will kill the man who hurt him. And then when I return, I'll deal with Kai. Because my father had it right the first time when he ordered me to kill her when we were teenagers. She has no business being in this life. And the only way to prevent her from winning is by killing her.

11

KAI

ENZO HATES ME.

And with good reason. I may have caused one of his only friends to die.

Enzo had said he considers Zeke and Langston to be family. But I didn't believe him until Langston carried Zeke inside lifeless in his arms. That's when I realized just how much Enzo cared for them.

I thought Enzo was heartless—I was wrong. He just doesn't care about me.

But he loves Zeke. He loves Langston. He loves his family.

And now Enzo's gone. To get revenge for hurting Zeke.

I never thought I'd be jealous of a dying man, but I am. Because Zeke was loved. And Enzo is going to make amends for what happened to Zeke.

When I was tortured, I got nothing. No revenge. No closure. *Nothing.*

I walk down the hallway cautiously searching for where the doctors brought Zeke. He looked so horrible when the doctors brought him in. Every inch of his clothes was caked in blood, and his gaping wounds were still bleeding, pouring more of his lifeline from his body until I'm not sure he had anything left.

If they save Zeke, it will be a miracle. Literally a miracle.

I knew it.

Langston knew it.

Enzo knew it.

The doctor saw it without even examining him.

Zeke is most likely already dead, and it's my fault.

I never thought I'd be ashamed of killing a man. Not after my trust in men was taken. But if Zeke dies, it will haunt me.

Why didn't I let Enzo go with them?

I'm not sure it would have made a difference other than Enzo might be lying side by side with Zeke, on death's doorstep. But it wouldn't be on my conscience. His death wouldn't be my fault.

Because I wanted to hurt Enzo.

I did hurt him—more than I ever bargained for.

I got my revenge on Enzo.

But I don't feel any better. Because as much as I'm pissed at Enzo for selling me, for being the catalyst that started this —Jarod was the one who hurt me every day. He's the one I hold responsible. Only when he's dead will I get my revenge.

I see Langston pacing outside of a closed door.

I don't know what to say, but I need to know, so I ask. "How is Zeke?"

Langston's head snaps so hard in my direction there was an audible sound to his hatred. With one look, Langston cuts to my core, ripping me open till I'm raw with emotion and pain.

I thought I knew torture and pain. It was nothing.

Knowing I hurt these men I thought were heartless and invincible kills me.

"He's dying. How do you think he is?" Langston barks.

"I'm sor—"

"I don't want to hear a pathetic apology from a bitch like you."

Langston had always been kind to me, but not now. Now he will hate me till the end of my days.

"Has the doctor said anything?" I ask, because I need to know.

He shakes his head. "He's in surgery."

"That's good. That means he's still alive."

"No, Enzo pays the doctor's so well they will fight for his life well beyond the length a normal doctor would give up and declare him dead. He could already be dead, and they will continue to work hours longer."

"There could be a miracle."

He glares at me. "A miracle would be if you dropped dead."

I suck in a breath at the invisible kick to the stomach.

"You're the reason he's in there! Do you understand that?"

I nod.

"I don't think you do! You prevented Enzo from going."

"I know, and I'm sorry, but Zeke would probably still be in there right now. Enzo would just be right in there with him."

"No." Langston hovers over me in an instant, and I wonder if he's going to slap me, grab me, or hit me. I deserve it, but I flinch, and he stops as if remembering what happened when he touched me the last time. How Enzo hurt him and threatened him never to do it again.

"Enzo wouldn't be in there. And Zeke wouldn't either.

You've never seen Enzo in action, so you don't understand. He's unstoppable. He can hear things, see things, sense things we can't. His intuition is unmatchable. He knows where and what our enemy is doing before they do.

"Zeke and I's connection to Enzo is strong. Once Enzo figures out a plan, it's almost instantaneous that he conveys it to Zeke and me. And with Zeke's strength, my quickness, and Enzo's power we are indomitable. We've been hurt, but never like this. We've never been so caught off guard. Never been this close to death before."

"He could still survive," I whisper, feeling Langston's pain with each word.

"You still don't understand. Zeke wasn't the only man who was hurt. He might be the closest to Enzo, but he isn't the only one. They killed over twenty men, injured more, and captured the rest. Those deaths are your fault."

The color drains from my face, and I collapse to the floor. I let men die.

"You should have let Enzo go. You aren't cut out for this world. You aren't even cut out to fight to become Black."

"I let Enzo go now," I say, finally looking up at Langston again.

"What do you mean?"

"He said there was nothing he could do for Zeke here. But he's going to get revenge. I let him go, but..." I can't finish. *Did I just send Enzo to his death?* Because the man that hurt Zeke like that will mutilate the man in charge.

And if Enzo is dead, that means I become Black by default.

Langston's right, I can't lead. I don't belong in this world. If I were to lead, the men would be dead within the month.

Enzo might be cruel, but I doubt every man who works for him deserves to die because of my incompetence. Men like my father work for Enzo, and as upset as I am at my father right now, I don't think he deserves to die.

"Good, Enzo will get revenge for Zeke." The way he says it makes it seem there is no way Enzo will die getting revenge. He says it like it's his word. Like it's already done.

Tears fall again as I shiver in my cold skin against the wall.

I did this.

Please come back Enzo. I don't want the empire. I don't want revenge. I don't want anyone else to die.

Langston paces while I shiver for several minutes before I gather my strength and stand. I'm no good quivering on the floor.

I fucked up; now I need to do everything I can to fix this.

Zeker is still in surgery, so there is nothing I can do for him.

Enzo is gone.

But Langston...he's in anguish.

He's beyond torn up, practically driving his feet so hard into the ground with each step I'm surprised he hasn't gone through the floorboards.

I can't help Zeke or Enzo, but I can help Langston.

I get up off the floor realizing for the first time I'm shirtless, only a bra covers my indecency. I gave up my top to help Zeke. My hands are covered in blood the same way Langston's are. The same Enzo's were.

I walk upstairs to the bathroom off the bedroom I share with Enzo and then wash my hands under the water, watching in horror as the water turns red from the blood of a man I can't save. Wiping the blood away in part feels like I'm washing him away.

Why do I care? Zeke was a monster. He killed men on a daily basis, but he didn't deserve to die.

When I'm finished washing, I mindlessly walk over to the closet, pull out a shirt and jeans, and put them on. Then I grab one of Enzo's shirts and jeans. They will be too big on Langston. Enzo is at least two inches taller, his muscles are more defined, but Langston needs a change of clothes. He can't keep walking around carrying his friend's blood on him all day.

I head downstairs and into the kitchen, trying to find a way to help Langston. I doubt he would take food. My stomach is in knots; his is probably worse.

He might drink booze, and it might help him numb his feelings, but I'm not sure if that's a good or bad thing.

Coffee.

It will warm him up and keep him awake while he waits for his friend.

"Miss Miller, can I help you with anything?" Westcott says.

"No, I got it."

"If you need any food or drink I would be happy to make it for you."

Westcott and I haven't always gotten along. He always seemed too cold and loyal to Enzo for my liking.

"Thank you, but I need to do this myself."

He gives me an understanding look, his eyes filled with sadness. "The coffee is in the cabinet on your right."

My mouth drops. *How did he know I was looking for coffee?* I think I've underestimated Westcott.

I turn to the cabinet and pull out the coffee. Of course, Enzo has a fancy coffee maker that takes me ten minutes to figure out how to use. But I do it. Then I pour the coffee into a mug and head back to Langston.

He's still pacing outside the door. It's started to get late into the middle of the night. But he's so awake I don't think he could sleep if he were forced to.

"Drink this," I say.

He ignores me.

"Langston, drink this," I try again, holding out the coffee.

"I'm not doing anything that brings me comfort, not while Zeke might be dying."

I huff. *Stubborn man.* They all are. "Drink this," I shove it into his hands. "You need it to stay awake and alert for Zeke."

I said the magic words, because he takes the mug from me without a thanks. He just stares a penetratingly dark gaze with his otherwise blue eyes.

"You need to change too," I say, holding out the clothes. If I hesitate, he might slap me for showing weakness.

"No."

I take a deep breath, trying to figure out how to approach it. "When Zeke awakes, you'll scare the shit out of him if he sees you coated in blood. He won't know if it's yours or his. Either way, it might put him into a shock. Change."

"Fine," he relents. He removes his shirt tossing it in my direction.

I try not to wince, but I can't help it.

He smiles smugly at my reaction.

He starts undressing his pants, and I don't react. I know what he's trying to do—goad me into to telling him he shouldn't undress in front of me. But I don't care. I just want him to feel better.

He kicks his jeans off, then does his best to wipe the blood from his hand on the jeans before throwing them at me.

Langston is ripped. He has thick thighs, a slender waist, and muscular arms. His body is marked with scars, similar to Enzo. Similar to my own marks. He just has fewer than me.

He smirks. "Like what you see, baby? Does my body turn you on, while my friend is dying? You know a good fuck might be the only thing that could cheer me up."

It's clear he doesn't want to fuck me, he's just trying to find any way to hurt me. So I ignore his disgusting comment.

"I'm sorry," I say.

He huffs.

I nod toward his scars. "This life has hurt us both, remember?" I glance down at my own scars covering my arms from the cuts and gunshots. "You've just been given a chance to have control; I haven't. I promise to you; I won't mess up again. I may not be able to bring Zeke or any of the other men back. But I promise to you I will live my life carrying that pain as I do these scars. And I will do everything in my power to right my wrong. If that means throwing the games on purpose to let Enzo win, I will. I promise."

Langston's eyes harden, and I think he's going to attack me. But then he exhales as if my words brought him some level of comfort.

I want to hug him, but I can't handle touch. And he's practically naked.

But I can see the pain. He needs comfort even if he won't accept it. Even if he will throw me across the room for my effort.

I hesitantly start toward him, not initially letting my actions known. Then when I get close, I wrap my arms around him quickly.

It feels like fire in my lungs at the touch. Uncontrollable pain surges through me as I hug him, but I don't let go.

Langston tries to fight me off, but I hold him tighter despite my own agony.

"I'm sorry. I don't want or expect you to ever forgive me. But I promise I will spend my life making up for any death I caused."

He tries again to free himself from my grip, and he could if he truly wanted to. Instead, I tighten, and he relents. He needs this hug.

I feel the heated tears on my shoulder. I feel his warm breath on my neck. Both should feel like comfort. Instead, they feel like tiny knives stabbing me over and over. But I don't let go.

He cries hard into my shoulder, his arms finally wrapping around me as he breaks for his friend—grieving for what he might lose.

Forever passes. Or at least that's how it feels to me. Like hell has engulfed me before Langston finally lets go.

His eyes are puffy and red, but he no longer looks at me like he wants to kill me—*that's a start.*

I pick up the clothes and hand them to him. He slowly takes them and starts dressing silently. When he finishes, he says, "You really can't stand being touched, can you?"

I open my eyes, realizing I haven't been able to look at him since I hugged him. My body shakes, icy sweat has soaked my body, and I'm frozen from the cold chill that has formed a layer over my skin trying to protect me from the evil.

"I can't."

"Then why did you do that?"

"Because you needed it."

His eyes soften, and I know he can't forgive me if his

friend dies, but he respects me for what I just did. For putting him above my own needs.

"Those men really hurt you, didn't they?"

I can't answer. "I'll go get you more coffee," I say, needing a minute to myself after what happened.

I return a few minutes later with more coffee for both of us. Even though I prefer iced, I drink the warm liquid trying to calm myself as I sit on the floor. Langston finally sits as well. Staring at me as often as he stares at the door that still hasn't opened.

"You should get a blanket. Warm yourself up. You were like ice to my touch."

I shake my head feeling the panic take hold of me. "I can't."

He frowns. "Are you too cold to move?"

"No, the blanket just won't help. It's a survival mechanism my body learned when I was taken. To shut down so I can't feel as much. My skin turns cold, my heart barely beats, so my organs need less oxygen to survive."

"I'll get you a blanket."

"No, the blanket won't help. The panic attack is too great. I won't be able to tolerate the touch right now."

"But you let Enzo touch you?"

I feel the water in my eyes. "Yes."

"Why?"

I chuckle gently. "I have no idea. I should hate him as much as he hates me."

Langston nods.

And then we are silent. We wait for the door to open. But it never does. With each minute that passes, I know the outcome—*Zeke's dead.*

Finally, the door opens and the doctor stands in the

doorway, covered in more blood than I knew was in a human body.

He's dead.

There is no way he survived this.

And with his death, I know I sealed my fate. Enzo will kill me for killing his friend. I've seen what he does to men who cross him. He will never forgive me for this.

Langston shoots up, but I remain seated. The fall will hurt less when I collapse from the pain if I'm already sitting.

"Did he?" Langston asks.

"Zeke's alive—for now."

He's alive.

12

ENZO

HE'S ALIVE.

That's the text message I received from Langston.

Zeke is alive.

I don't know for how long. I don't know if he will survive for another hour, another day, another week. Or if he's out of the worst of it.

But he's alive.

I grin, which means I can bring Zeke vengeance while he is still breathing. He will know I killed the man who did this to him before he breathes his last breath. Or he'll know when he finally opens his eyes and decides to rejoin the living.

Either way, it's what I've been needing to hear.

My heart aches a little less knowing Zeke is still alive. The tightness in my chest has loosened, which will make it easier to do the job I'm about to do. But my anger hasn't, which won't bode well for Billy, Alastar's right-hand man and the man who tried to maim Zeke. After doing some digging into Alastar's crew, I learned Billy was the most likely culprit of Zeke's wounds. They use our security equipment, so I was able to hack the system and get security footage. Billy was the fucker who hurt Zeke.

I climb up the ladder of the yacht Billy calls his home. My veins pumped with excitement when I realized he's at sea. I prefer to do my work here on the sea rather than back on land. I feel more alive on the water.

I didn't bring any of my men with me. I would never ask them to seek my revenge. Never put them in danger when I can handle the threat myself.

That's one of the reasons the name Black has become even more of a legend since I took over. My father was evil, killing men who didn't deserve to die. I, on the other hand, am fair, but when someone crosses one of my men, clients, or me, they pay with their life.

Killing Billy won't be enough. I need to make an example of him so no other man will ever cross me. And the world will know Black is still alive and well. That marrying Kai didn't make me weak, if anything, it made me stronger.

I thought pretending Kai was my wife would make me appear stronger, but it hasn't. I'm about to remedy the situation—by telling the world the truth. She's mine by force, not willingly. The only person to ever be told differently was Dallas, and he's dead now. The rest of the world has heard rumors I've married, which is why I was attacked. They will know the truth. She's my slave, nothing more.

Kai thinks I've mistreated her in the past. She has no idea what I'm truly capable of. She will be my slave in every sense. She deserves to feel the pain of hurting someone I love.

But for now, I need to focus on my current task.

My feet hit the top deck silently. The security on the ship is of the highest caliber. Alastar is wealthy and will ensure his men take no precautions. They have too many enemies to not be secure at all times.

But he forgets I invented most of the security he uses. The cameras are mine. The alarms are mine. Even the men who work for him were trained in my ways, the man I'm hunting included.

So getting around the security team is easy enough.

But I don't want to get around the security system. I don't want to go unhidden. I want to slaughter any man who dared to cross me.

So instead of sneaking through the ship to the main panel to shut off the cameras, I make my presence known immediately.

I remove my dark jacket, letting the white of my shirt underneath light up on the cameras.

"You want me! I'm here!" I say into the night, knowing every man on this yacht has been notified of my existence and is making plans to take me out.

They should. They should shoot me in the head on the spot instead of trying to torture me into telling them what they want to know.

But they are too stupid and cocky. They think a dozen men can easily hold me back while they torture me.

I silently laugh. They have no idea. No idea the training my father put me through. No idea what I'm capable of given the right motivation.

The men descend as I expect them to, with weapons drawn all aimed at me.

"Drop your weapons!" one man yells in my direction.

I don't even have a weapon out, but they already see me as a threat.

I slowly reach into my pants and produce my gun. I hold it up to them, then drop it on the floor, my heart racing fast not from the fear but in anticipation of what I know is coming.

"Put your hands up."

So predictable.

I do.

And then two men grab my arms, forcing them behind my back as they start walking me brutally forward.

They don't even bother tying my wrists together. They think two large men holding me with dozens of guns aimed at me is enough—they have no idea.

I'm walked down into the depths of the yacht—to their leader, Billy.

It's exactly what I want. I will kill these men for who they work for. But Billy is who I want. He's the one who tortured Zeke. He's the one who ordered Zeke to die because I wasn't there to torture instead.

Billy isn't the leader, but he is the leader of this ship. Similar in rank to Zeke. It's only fair that I repay him with the same scars he caused Zeke—the same pain. But unlike Zeke, he won't be surviving the night.

The door opens, and I'm shoved inside with the two men still twisting my arms behind my back roughly, like that is going to force me to do what they say. I can still feel the metal of their guns pointed on me from behind, but I don't give a shit about any of them.

I care about the man standing in front of me—Billy.

"I didn't think you'd be stupid enough to set foot on my ship, Black. Not after what I did to your man," Billy says not bothering to rise from his seat.

I smile smugly. *This will be too easy.*

"I just thought I'd repay you for your hospitality the last time you hosted one of my men."

His eyes darken. "It will be I who shows you the same hospitality I showed your man."

I growl roughly. "I'm giving you one chance, Billy. Save your men. Surrender to me now, and I'll let them live. I'll even give them a chance to change their loyalty and work for me. If not, they will all die."

"It will be you who dies after you tell us what we want to know."

"And what is that?"

"We want what everyone wants. We want the power of Black. We want to be granted the title. We know the title is earned, not born into. When we kill you, we will earn it."

I laugh. "You want to know if killing me is enough to grant you the title? You don't know the ways of my organization. There is only one way you become Black, and that isn't it. You can kill me, but it won't solve your problem. Black will just be reborn again, with a leader just as ruthless as I am." If I die, Kai becomes the leader. And that scares the shit out of me.

"Then we want to know how to destroy you. We want the codes to your bank accounts. We want a list of your allies. We want the blueprints to your security systems."

"You can't destroy Black. Even if you were to torture and kill me, you would be no better off than you are now. In fact, you'd be worse off if you killed me, because the new Black would be pissed. He'd take over, and his first task would be to hunt you down and kill you, slowly. You're lucky I'm here."

"Why's that?"

"Because I intend to kill you quickly. Zeke's alive, and I want to go back and tell him the good news that I've killed you."

That's when I make my move. I jerk my arms, not caring

if they pull my arms out of their sockets. The sudden twist of my arms brings the men on either side of me to my knees because they refuse to let me go. Refusing to let me go will be their deaths.

I dive behind one, as the bullets start raining, killing the first man. Then I grab the other and slit his throat with the knife they never took from my pocket.

Like I would board a hostile enemy's yacht with only one weapon—idiots.

I take his gun and start shooting. The men start retreating down the hallway. I slam the door I know is bulletproof and invincible to attack. I built this yacht after all. I know the security. I know Billy would keep the most secure room for himself.

And now he's trapped. His men can't get in, but they will hear his screams and know they are next. Some might even go overboard and swim for shore rather than let me kill them.

Billy's eyes go wide in fear. He may be the leader. He may be used to torturing and killing people, but he doesn't usually get involved in a fight until the enemy has been weakened.

He's used to hurting men who are already injured and weak. Men who are tied up, making them easy to torture.

I wipe the blood from my knife on my jeans. I want a fresh knife when I cut and dice him like he did Zeke.

"What do you want?" he already asks, his voice wavering with fear.

I smirk. "Already trying to bargain for your life, Billy? We haven't even gotten started yet."

"I have money; you can have it all."

Jesus, this man is pathetic. He'll be pissing his pants before I'm done with him.

"Don't do the crime if you can't do the time, Billy."

"I didn't. I didn't touch your friend."

I shake my head in disgust of this man.

"Lying, that's not going to save you."

I take a step forward, holding the knife loosely in my hand.

His eyes dart around the room, in search of an escape.

I wait for him to draw his weapon, but then I realize what he is looking for—a weapon.

I chuckle. "You are the worst. You don't even have a weapon on you at all times, do you?"

I toss him the gun I'm holding. "You get one shot, so you better make it good."

He barely catches the metal, bobbling it before gripping it like his life depends on it.

It does.

His hand trembles, and he fires in my direction without steadying it.

I don't even have to dive out of the way to avoid the path of the bullet, that's how far he missed.

"You missed." My lips curl into a devilish grin. "My turn."

I disarm him with ease. Then my knife presses hard into his chest, mimicking the first wound he caused Zeke.

Billy cries out from the plunge of my knife into his lungs.

"It hurts, doesn't it? Soon you'll have trouble getting oxygen into those lungs because of the gaping hole."

I pull on the knife then stab into the other side of his chest. His hand reaches up to try to stop me, but I bat it down like it's a fly.

"Oh, don't cry. We are just getting started. I haven't even got to the good part yet."

I stab him hard into his stomach, twisting to create as much damage as possible.

"I'm being kinder than you were, Billy. You used a gun to create most of the wounds on Zeke. A bullet that exploded into his body. My knife goes in and out cleanly. It's more personal this way." The blood from his body oozes everywhere, and if I weren't holding him up, he'd have collapsed to the floor already.

His body jerks forward, trying to collapse from weakness.

"Not yet, you don't get to die yet."

He moans and cries.

"Please."

"Please what?"

"Just let me die."

I crack my neck. This is the best part—when you've finally broken them. They no longer wish for life, just death. Because not existing is better than living.

"Do you remember the last thing you did, Billy?"

"No," he moans.

"Then let me remind you. After you shot him multiple times, you beat him. But I don't have time for that, and you are too weak to survive. You tied his hands behind his back so he couldn't fight back. You had men holding him so he couldn't fight instead of facing him one on one like a man. Then you tried to castrate him."

He shakes in my grasp. "Please."

"You missed; I won't."

I stab him in the groin as he cries like the biggest pussy alive. I release him and let him crumple to the floor, but his screams don't stop. Every man aboard the ship hears his cries. And if they weren't terrified before, they are now.

The blood spills out of Billy quickly as I stand over him.

He got off easy if you ask me. Because within a few seconds, he's dead.

I pick up the gun and head to the door to kill the rest of his men. Once I'm done, word will spread of what happened here. The Black name will be restored.

Then all I have left to do is deal with Kai for risking Zeke's life in the first place. I've never been so happy about punishing someone before. It will cement her hatred for me, but it's necessary.

No one goes unpunished—least of all Kai. I've been thinking of her as a weakling who I needed to treat with careful movements because of the pain she's been through.

But the second she signed the papers, wanting to become Black, the game started. And I can no longer treat her like a princess. She wants to be in this world; then she gets to live with the consequences of her decisions. And I don't regret that I'm going to enjoy punishing her.

13

KAI

I've LOST the right to see how Zeke is, so I don't enter the room when the doctor talks to Langston about Zeke's condition. Langston may respect me, but he hasn't forgiven me. I might have a chance at forgiveness now that Zeke has survived, but that won't come for a long time.

The doctor tells Langston that if Zeke survives the night, he will have an excellent chance at living.

I listen as Langston goes to his friend and cries gently at the possibility that his friend could die.

The doctors and nurses that treated Zeke file out of the room. The lead doctor stops when he sees me. "I'll make sure a nurse is always awake monitoring Zeke through the worse of it. I'll send most of my team home, but I'd like to stay in case something happens I can take him back into surgery quickly. Is there a place I can freshen up and get some rest?"

He talks to me like I own this house—like I could make such a decision. I will never make a decision again after what happened to Zeke.

The doctor sees the pain in my eyes. "I don't make assurances I can't keep. But Zeke is a fighter. I've stopped the bleeding and gave him a blood transfusion. I mended the broken bones. He has a real shot at surviving."

I shake my head. "It's not that..."

He sighs. "I never ask questions or get involved in my high profile client's lives. But I can tell you, this isn't your fault."

"It is," I say sternly. I will feel this pain for the rest of my life because I almost caused him to die. "Westcott will see you to a room," I say, hoping the man is behind me as usual.

"Follow me this way, Dr. Patten," Westcott says.

I sit on the floor outside of Zeke's room, knowing I can't enter, but also that I can't leave. I need to know Zeke is okay. I need to apologize to him, but I won't as long as Langston is there.

I listen to Langston talk to Zeke even though he's still out. "I'm so sorry. It should have been me. I wish I could trade places with you." He really does love him like a brother.

I smile. I wish someone loved me like that. But I don't have anyone. My father lied to me my whole life. I have no siblings. Mason likes me, but we didn't have this kind of connection. Not one where we'd give our lives to save the other.

I have no one.

I hug my knees, feeling alone. I hate being alone.

"Miss Miller, you should get some sleep. Mr. Black wouldn't like to know you aren't taking care of yourself," Westcott says.

"Mr. Rinaldi wants me dead for what I did. I don't think he cares if I sleep or not," I say, never letting Westcott forget Enzo hasn't earned the Black title yet.

Westcott sighs. "Mr. Rinaldi is a complicated man. I think you should sleep."

"I can't." The tears fall as I look at the closed door that leads to Zeke. "I won't be able to sleep until Zeke is up and walking on his own."

"That could take weeks."

"Then, that's how long I'll wait."

Westcott must realize arguing with me right now will lead nowhere. So he leaves me to sit quietly outside Zeke's door, alone.

Hours pass, and eventually, Langston stops talking.

A new nurse arrives, and I stand, peaking my head inside as the nurses change shifts. I see Langston passed out in the chair next to Zeke's bed.

I enter cautiously, like Langston might wake and drive me away.

He doesn't. He snores loudly, utterly exhausted as he sleeps in the oversized chair.

The room is set up like a hospital room in one half; the other half a makeshift surgery room.

"Do you know if there are any extra pillows or blankets in here?" I ask the nurse.

She smiles and walks to the closet retrieving one of both for me.

"Thanks," I say.

She studies the machines around where Zeke lays, while I cover Langston with the blanket and slip the pillow behind his head so his neck won't be sore when he wakes.

"I'll give you some privacy," the nurse says.

"No, you don't need to do that."

"Don't worry." She holds up her computer. "All the machines are hooked up so I can monitor him from my laptop. And if you need anything, just press the button over his bed and it will alert me."

I nod as she leaves.

I pull a chair up next to Zeke's bed and study him. He looks so lifeless it's hard to believe he is truly alive. Except for the rise and fall of his chest, he looks like a corpse. His face is white, his body still, and tubes jet into his broken arms and legs. Bandages cover what I can see of his head and arms, and I can only imagine what his chest and legs look like beneath the covers.

I reach out and touch his hand, shocked at the initial pain of the touch, but I push through it to comfort him. He doesn't stir. "I'm sorry. I'm so sorry," I say as tears fall.

"I never meant for anyone to get hurt. I was just trying to hurt Enzo for selling me. You were never supposed to get hurt—I'm sorry."

Zeke doesn't react to my words. He just lays lifeless.

And I don't want him to forgive me for what I did anyway. So I just hold his hand hoping he knows how sorry I am.

Zeke's body starts writhing beneath the blankets.

"Zeke," I say hesitantly, seeing him stir.

"Zeke, it's okay. No one can hurt you."

His eyes fly open as his body jolts. And then I realize what's happening—pain.

He must be in incredible pain.

"Squeeze my hand as hard as you need." I reach up and press the button for the nurse. "The nurse will bring you more pain medication."

Langston wakes up from the noise. When he sees me, he stills, "What are you doing? What did you do to him?"

"He's waking up. I called the nurse. I'm just trying to keep him calm until he gets more pain medication."

Zeke moans, and Langston forgets about me. He grabs his friend's hand. "It's okay. I'm here. You're going to be fine."

The nurse rushes in.

"He woke up, and he's in a lot of pain," I say.

"I'll get him more pain medication," she says, racing toward the cart with the meds.

"No," Zeke says.

We all turn to him as he says his first words. Both happy and confused at his choice of words. "I don't want any medication. I don't want to be knocked out again."

"You're safe. No one can hurt you. Enzo went to get your revenge. Take the drugs, man," Langston says.

Zeke shakes his head, and the nurse stops.

Zeke moans again, biting his lip to keep the curses in as another wave of torment hits him.

"Give him the fucking drugs!" Langston screams at the nurse.

"I can't go against the patient's wishes."

"Dammit, Zeke, if you don't let the nurse give you the drugs I'll do it myself," Langston says.

This is getting us nowhere, so I speak up. "We won't leave you, Zeke. Not for a second. One of us will hold your hand even if the drugs knock you out again. But you need the drugs to heal. Your body is in too much pain; you could go into shock and die from the pain—that's not fair to Enzo or Langston. They both love you, and you need to survive for them. Let the nurse do her job. We promise as soon as it's safe, we will reduce the medication so you can stay awake."

Zeke watches my mouth studying it closely like my mouth holds the key to his decision.

Finally, Zeke nods at the nurse.

"Give him the drugs," Langston says as Zeke's grip on both of our hands tighten as his face scrunches in agony.

The nurse gives him drugs through his IV, and within moments Zeke is calm and quiet again. His eyes slowly flutter closed until he's out again.

Langston looks to me and gives me a nod instead of a thank you. But I didn't do it for him. I did it because Zeke needed it.

Langston's phone buzzes and he looks at it and curses.

"I have to go," he says as he stares at his buddy.

"Go, I'll stay. I promise I won't stop holding his hand or sleep until you return."

"Fuck," Langston says pacing back and forth.

"Go," I say again, holding Zeke's hand tighter. Langston studies my grip on his hand. He knows it causes me pain, but this is my penance. I'll hold his hand all night to comfort him no matter how painful it is for me.

Langston disappears without another word. I don't know what drew him away, but I know it must be serious. Langston wouldn't leave otherwise.

Enzo?

Could Enzo be hurt? It's the only thing I can think of that would cause Langston to leave.

My eyes water again thinking of Enzo hurt like Zeke. I can't imagine it. He's too strong to be injured. Too much of a king to lay lifeless on the ground with blood seeping from his body. But he's human. It could happen.

And I shouldn't care. I should dance on Enzo's grave the second he dies.

But I wouldn't.

I don't understand why, but I care about Enzo. I twirl the ring on my finger.

Don't you dare be hurt Enzo. Don't make me a fake widower.

I continue to hold Zeke's hand through the night and next day. The doctor returns to check on him and smiles when he sees me.

"You love him?" he asks.

I shake my head as I stare at Zeke. "Not like that." I'm not capable of love. And I'm afraid the only man I could possibly even love is the man who also sold me. *How fucked up is that?* He's the only man I can touch without feeling pain. He's the only one capable of stealing my heart.

"How is he doing?" I ask.

"Good. His vitals are strong. He's a fighter. I'll have the nurse lower his meds so he can wake up soon. I can't say with certainty, but I can say confidently he will live."

"Thank you, doctor."

The doctor leaves, and the nurse gives him a new medication to help him start waking up.

Zeke's eyes open and this time the pain has softened.

"Thank you," he says.

"No, don't thank me. I'm the reason you are in this mess. I'm so sorry for letting you get hurt. But you don't need to talk—just rest. Langston and Enzo will be back as soon as they can. They are ensuring you get revenge."

The nurse comes over, helps him drink, and makes sure he's comfortable before leaving us by ourselves.

He stares at my hand. "Have you been holding my hand all night?"

"Yes, as I promised earlier."

He studies me closely. "Even though it brings you great pain to touch me?"

"Yes, I deserve the pain. And I wanted to comfort you."

He grips my hand tighter to see how badly it affects me and a tear rolls down. He softens his grip immediately but doesn't let go.

"Thank you," he says again.

This time I don't argue.

"I'm so sorry, Zeke. I will never let it happen again. Enzo will make all the decisions when it comes to Surrender and the men. And I will do whatever I can to make it up to you."

Zeke shakes his head. "It's not your fault."

"It is."

"No, it's not."

I frown.

"I'm glad Enzo wasn't there. More than likely I wouldn't be lying in this bed if he were, he's strong, fearless, and smarter than any of our enemies, but I don't mind taking a bullet or two for Enzo. God knows, he's taken too many bullets for me."

"But he wouldn't have had to, if he had gone. If I had let him go, all of the men would be alive and well. You wouldn't be here. And Enzo wouldn't be hurt either. He would have protected you."

"Probably, but it still isn't your fault."

"Then whose fault is it?"

"Enzo's."

I shake my head. "No."

"Yes, if anyone is to blame it's him. But I don't blame him. This isn't his fault. He was just protecting those he cares about."

"I don't understand."

"The man who hurt you..."

"Jarod."

"Yes, Jarod. Do you know what happened to him?"

I shrug. "I assume he still sails on his yacht, taking on new women as slaves in every port and fucking them until he kills them."

"No, he doesn't."

I freeze; my body, heart, and soul stop.

"Enzo hunted Jarod down. We snuck onto his yacht. And Enzo tortured and then killed him for what he did to you."

I gasp. *Why? Why would he do that?* He sold me to him. He wanted me ruined, hurt, broken.

Zeke reads my eyes. "Enzo is loyal to the ones who are loyal to him. He protects those he views as innocent. And he gets revenge for those he loves."

"He doesn't love me."

"No, maybe not. But he does care about you."

Enzo cares about me. He got revenge for me. He protected me.

"I may not understand the relationship you two have. I don't understand why he would sell you only to keep you safe here, but don't ever forget he cares about you and will always care about you. That's why he stayed instead of coming to protect us. He won't hurt you."

"Don't make promises I have no intentions of keeping," Enzo says from behind me.

My heart sputters—happy Enzo is alive and afraid of what he will do. Enzo may have cared before, but I betrayed him by not letting him save his friend. He won't forgive me for that. I know because no matter what his intentions were when he sold me, I can't forgive him.

You can only truly forgive those you love, and we will never love each other.

14

ENZO

SHE'S HOLDING his fucking hand.

Like that is going to absolve her of her sins.

Her eyes smile at me when she first spots me, as if I'm her favorite person and she's happy to see me. But as soon as she sees the pain etched, the lines formed from worry now hardened into rage, her smile drops.

And Kai can't hide the agony streaming through her body as she holds Zeke's hand. Every part of her body is begging her to let go. Her mind is screaming, her heart pumping wildly trying to get her to flee. She holds her hand calm in Zeke's, but the rest of her body is on edge as if Zeke's a lion about to attack her.

Good. She deserves every drop of pain she's feeling. She's responsible for Zeke's condition in the first place.

But when my gaze turns to Zeke, he looks happy, content. Sure, he's in pain from his injuries, but it's like her touch comforts him.

He's fucking forgiven her.
Shit.

How the hell did that happen? Doesn't he realize she's the reason he almost died?

Zeke raises an eyebrow as if to challenge my assumptions about Kai.

I shake my head, not believing he could forgive her. I'll deal with that later. Right now, I need to know he's truly going to make it.

"How are you feeling?" I ask, making sure to stay clear of Kai as I walk to the other side of his bed.

"Like I was shot multiple times," Zeke answers.

"Yea, you look like shit, man," I say, with a grin.

He grins back. "You don't look too good yourself."

I stare down at my blood covered clothes. I didn't want to change until he saw the proof for himself.

"Did you get the bastard?" Zeke asks.

"You know I did."

"Good." Zeke's eyes face forward, and a cloud of gloom glazes over them as if he was back on that yacht reliving the attack all over again.

Kai squeezes his hand, noticing the change. It takes a minute, but Zeke eventually breathes normally again as he gives her a tight smile of thanks.

Jesus, she can't be helping him right now.

"Zeke, you're awake," Langston says from the doorway.

Zeke smiles at Langston, and it finally feels like home having us all here together again.

Langston surveys the room, then he spots Kai, and he fucking smiles at her too.

Does no one see how she betrayed us? How holding Zeke's hand does nothing to earn our forgiveness? She needs to be punished for what she did.

"Did you kill him?" Langston asks.

"Yes, I declared war against Alastar and his men. But

after the message I sent in torturing and killing Billy, they would be wise to surrender now instead of fighting."

We all grin and nod. This is when we are our best, when we are together.

But then their smiles begin to include Kai.

No—fucking no!

She isn't one of us. She's the enemy. She will never be one of us. All she'll end up doing is getting one of us killed.

I won't let either of them die because of her.

Kai senses that I'm breaking, losing my cool. And it's time for her to face her punishment for hurting Zeke.

She squeezes Zeke's hand one last time and then looks to Langston who immediately takes her place at Zeke's bedside before she stands up walking toward me with her head high, ready to face her punishment.

Relenting won't make her punishment any easier on her. In fact, it might make it worse.

She walks out of the room first, and I follow. Zeke and Langston both know what I'm about to do, but I won't do it in front of them. Not when they have taken a liking to Kai. But they won't stop this from happening. If either of them had betrayed us, then I would have punished them all the same.

I close the door to Zeke's room behind us calmly, as if I'm not about to explode.

"Enzo, I'm sorr—"

I glare at her.

She stops speaking.

Then, I start walking.

I can't do this here. Not so close to Zeke. He has too big of a heart. If he hears her screaming, he'll tell Langston to stop me.

So I walk upstairs to my bedroom, which I know is

soundproof. Kai follows, walking like a prisoner about to go to the gallows.

I expected a fight, but apparently, she agrees she should be punished.

I hold the door open to my bedroom and wait for her to walk through. Then I slam the door shut.

She jumps at the noise.

"Enzo—"

"Don't. There is nothing you can say."

She crosses her arms across her chest looking at me defiantly.

"I should kill you," I say.

"You won't."

I hate how confidently she says I won't kill her. But then I should have killed her when we were teenagers, and I didn't. I won't do it now either. I can't. She knows it, I know it.

"I won't." *That would be too easy.*

She exhales as if she didn't fully believe I wouldn't kill her until this very moment.

"You killed Jarod?" she asks.

"Yes."

"Thank you," she whispers, with tears in her eyes—tears of forgiveness. I could be forgiven so easily if I just told her the truth. She's so close to giving it to me anyway, even if I don't fully deserve it.

But I don't want her forgiveness.

Just like she doesn't deserve mine.

We've both hurt each other too many times for forgiveness to ever be an option.

"I wouldn't do it again. I've saved you too many times."

She narrows her gaze at my cruel words. "Stop pretending you are a monster when you aren't."

"You don't think I'm a monster?"

"Not as often as you are a protector."

I shake my head. "I'm about to remedy that thought. Because I am most definitely a monster. I'm not going to kill you, but I am going to punish you. And when the games start, I'm going to destroy you."

I grab her by the neck and slam her body into the wall.

She doesn't cry out; her body knows how to protect her from pain even though it's screaming out in pain from my touch around her throat. I've barely squeezed yet, and she already can't stand me.

"Punish me, you bastard, but don't think I won't punish you right back."

I laugh. "You have nothing you can punish me with."

She gives me a wicked look. "Yes, I do."

"No, you don't. You're too weak to punish me physically. I know you think you have Zeke and Langston wrapped around your little finger, but it's not enough. They won't hurt me, no matter what you want them to do."

"I know Zeke and Langston wouldn't lay a hand against you."

"Neither would Westcott or Archard or any of the men at the club. Your father won't; he'd lose his job and his life. And you don't have any friends to help you."

She looks hurt at my last statement. But it's the truth. She has no one.

"I don't need anyone to help me extract my punishment."

"Yes, you do." I squeeze tighter around her throat until she can barely breathe.

Stop.

My conscious comes back with a vengeance. *Stop, you aren't a monster.* You have to save her from yourself, or nothing you've done will be worth it. You will become the one thing you've worked your whole life not to be—*your father.*

"I could snuff the life out of you with just my hand."

"But you won't," she croaks barely getting enough oxygen to talk. She should be terrified. But instead, she licks her lips then parts them practically welcoming me to do what I want with her body.

Because I want her.

I have no self-control left. I want her body. I want to dive into the depths of her body and claim every inch of her. I want to be the only one who can touch her. I want to bring her pleasure, not because she deserves it, but because no other man has. And then I want to punish her ass for letting my friend get hurt.

But you did the same thing. You let her get hurt.

And I've gotten revenge for her. I saved her life. And I've kept her alive here. I protected her. I kept her safe. And I've punished myself plenty, but I know it's not enough. I deserve to be punished the same as her.

I'll let her, but first I need to punish her. I need to get the image of Zeke's lifeless body out of my head. I need to heal my bleeding heart.

"Punish me, Enzo. I deserve it. But don't think I won't punish you as soon as you're finished for what you've done to me."

15

KAI

HE THINKS he can punish me. *He can't.*

I've suffered every possible torture imaginable.

I've been shot, beaten, stabbed, whipped; the list goes on.

And it wasn't just physical pain; it was psychological. I suffered alone. I suffered without any comforting touch for years. I went without food. I went without light.

I adapted. My body learned to shut down like a bear hibernates to survive the winter. My body learned to lock itself away only leaving the most vital of organs functioning.

No one can truly hurt me.

Yes, I don't like people's touch, but I can handle it. I've held Zeke's hand for the last eight hours. It's not a picnic, but I can endure it.

Yes, I don't like the water or boats, but Enzo threw me into the water, and I survived only suffering through a frantic heartbeat.

Yes, I don't like the light, but I've learned to live in the light as easily as I breathe in the dark.

Yes, I don't like a soft bed, but I've learned to sleep on a blanket of pillows as easily as a hard floor.

Enzo can't hurt me. Whatever punishment he has planned, I can endure. I can survive. I will take the scars in and come out stronger.

And I know how Enzo wants to punish me.

I can see the lust shining in the dark irises of his eyes. It's the same feeling we've both had since six years ago when we first met. And tonight, we will finish what should have started then.

We have a connection—neither of us can deny it.

But it's a connection neither of us understands.

Is the connection because we were both destined to be enemies from the start?

Is it because he was born in the dark and I the light?

Or did it grow as we both realized the other was untouchable?

We are going to find out. We are going to put an end to the tension between us.

He wants to use sex to punish me—and I want him to.

It was inevitable we would eventually fuck. He's the only man in my life. The only person who can touch me without me flinching. The only person I've ever thought of naked.

We've seen each other naked. We are both attracted to each other. We both want each other.

And this is how it has to happen. *As punishment—rough, primal, carnal.*

I don't want it any other way.

If we go slow, trying to ease me into it, I'll back out. It will give me too much time to think about what I'm doing and how wrong it feels. I can't let my brain think about what's happening. It just needs to happen.

This is the way.

Sex will either heal me or break me—maybe both.

We've tried for weeks now, and there is this constant pull back to each other. But once we've finally fucked we will be free. To forgive each other for our past sins. To be the enemies we were always destined to be.

"Punish me, fuck me," I say as he continues to grip my neck. The last time he did this was on a yacht, and we ended up going overboard. His decision then changed my life, as will his decision now. But I have more control now than I ever realized. And I have my own punishment in mind for Enzo.

Once we fuck, we will be even. All will be forgiven, because I can't keep living with the pain. And neither can he. It will consume us. And we both need to be ready for when the games start.

He narrows his gaze as his fingers tighten around my neck until only the tiniest slip of oxygen can make it to my lungs.

"Don't ask for something you can't handle," he growls.

"I. Can. Handle. It."

He bites his lip as if it's taking all of his self-control to hold himself back. His eyes go back and forth as he searches for the answer. Because as much as he wants me, he won't rape me. As much as I've branded him the devil, there is a part of him that isn't.

The world Enzo grew up in was different than mine. He did horrible things in the name of survival. And that hardened him, but there is still a part of the boy inside of him that has hope for something better. Something that isn't so dark and cruel.

And that part of him is the part I will break. Only then will we be even.

"How, when you can barely handle Zeke's touch? How, when you've only just accepted my touch?"

I try to take a deep breath but I can't. My head is dizzy with lack of oxygen. "Because I want it. I want you to fuck me."

"Liar."

This is going to be hard, convincing him to use sex as punishment. I need to piss him off enough so it's the only option in his mind.

"If not then what? You're going to whip me? Beat me?"

"Maybe."

A whipping or beating would be easy for me to tolerate. It's happened countless times. And I know Enzo is mad for getting Zeke hurt, almost killed, but the beating would be nothing compared to Jarod's.

But if he beat me, I couldn't get my revenge.

"So you'll beat me, but you won't rape me?" I spit out.

His eyes darken. "I don't hurt women."

"No, you don't rape them. That's not who you are. You aren't like your father," I say, guessing that his father is a sensitive subject.

He growls. *I guessed right.*

"And beating me, wouldn't be hurting me?"

He glares and tightens then loosens his grip all in the span of a second as if he's arguing with himself about what to do.

Now's my chance.

"Langston did."

"What?" his grip instantly constricts.

"Langston fucked me," I lie, remembering Langston's threat when he was so vengeful and stunned.

He blinks rapidly, not understanding my words.

"I was aching and desperate to feel good after what

happened to Zeke. We got lost in the moment, and he fucked me. It was good. Hot, thrilling, passionate. That's how I got him to forgive me, by fucking him like the whore I am."

Pain, anger, rage.

I see it all in his eyes. He's pissed at Langston for touching me, but he's livid at me.

"You aren't the only man who can touch me. If a man earns it, then it doesn't hurt me. Langston did. And his cock—"

"Shut up," his voice booms.

He squeezes until I can't get any oxygen in. My lies work. They prompt him to use sex instead of a whip.

"He wouldn't fuck you."

I raise an eyebrow, still unable to speak. He loosens his grip.

"Langston fucked me. Truth or lie?" I ask.

His face reddens, and the veins on his arms pop.

"Stop distracting me from punishing you. You deserve to be punished for putting Zeke at risk, so you won't do it again."

"I agree. Fuck me, Enzo. Punish me," I taunt.

His eyes darken as he tries to read my body. Attempts to give me one last time to choose a different route. He takes a deep breath trying to control his breathing like he controls everything else in his life. But I just offered him the one thing he's been dying for on a silver platter. And once he starts, he will lose all of his self-control. And the possibility that I willingly fucked another man other than him is driving him mad.

I will hold power. But I will be trading my body to get it.

"Fuck me and find out if I'm telling the truth or if I'm a liar."

"If I fuck you, it will hurt. The only pleasure you will get is when I make you come but only after you've paid your penance," he says, trying one last attempt to stop me from letting him fuck me.

I grin. *This is what I want.* A man practically begging me to fuck him. A man whose desire I can feel taking hold of all the air in the room. There is no doubt in my mind how much Enzo wants me—for me. Not because he thinks of me as a whore. He wants my body, but he also wants all of me. His intentions are clear. He wants to fuck and control me. He just doesn't realize he will be giving me just as much control as he'll be receiving.

And I want him just as much in return. He's not like those monsters who held me captive for years. Enzo is beyond attractive. I've seen him naked. His body is better than any flawless statue of a Greek God. He has thick muscles, a chiseled jaw, and defined abs. *What more could a woman want?*

He's fierce, formidable, and powerful. No one would ever call Enzo weak. And after seeing how he cares about the men he calls family, I've never been so turned on by someone who could be so protective of those he loves. Whoever finally steals his heart and persuades him to marry her will be a lucky woman.

"I'm not looking for pleasure; I'm looking for punishment." I mean every word. Sex will never be pleasurable for me. I'm too fucked up for that. But maybe it can be exciting, thrilling, and dangerous. Maybe with the right man, I can learn to relax enough to enjoy it. And Enzo is the only chance I have of learning to push through it.

My words cut through his dark exterior. And I see a glimpse of the man who is more than a ruthless leader, but the man who is kind, gentle, caring. A man I would love to

154

get to know more, but I never will. After we fuck, we will cement ourselves as enemies with the sexual frustration no longer hanging us down.

"I could make it as pleasurable as you want, Kai. You've never been with a man who wants to make it good for you. A man who knows your body better than you know yourself. If I wanted to, you would enjoy every moment of this."

"But you don't. You want to hurt and punish me—you're the same as Jarod."

His jaw tenses, his hand closes around my throat, and heat pours from his body. "I am nothing like Jarod. I killed that bastard, for you. You should have never been sold to such a heartless man. That was my mistake."

I still, trying to preserve what little oxygen I have while he tightens on my neck. *I will not show fear.*

"Your first time after Jarod should be all euphoria. It should be slow and gentle and kind. It should be healing—this won't be."

"This isn't my first time," I lie.

The promise in his eyes is exactly what I want. This will be rough, and unforgiving.

I try to speak but I can't. He releases me. "I know. Fuck me, how you've always wanted to, Enzo. I need to be punished. I need to be fucked, not made love to with gentle hands in order to forgive myself." *I need this to heal.*

He doesn't give me another chance to change my mind.

He releases me and steps back, while I cough, my throat burning from lack of oxygen and his fingers squeezing my neck.

"Kneel," he says.

I raise an eyebrow. Now that we are doing this, my mind is going a million miles a minute thinking about all the things he could want from me. How he will torture me for almost getting his friend killed.

"Kneel, Kai. If I have to ask you again, you won't come even after I'm finished punishing you. You will hate me and hate sex, forever. I will ruin you."

I kneel immediately. This is what I agreed to. Doing whatever he said. Letting him control how and when we fuck.

Trust him. Trust him not to ruin you.

I look up at him with big eyes as he takes a step toward me in his jeans and dark T-shirt. The man he killed's blood still speckles his clothes.

He undoes his jeans and reaches inside.

Fuck, are we doing this right away? No foreplay? No kisses? Nothing? Just straight to fucking?

He pulls his large, thick cock out. And I stare at his cock eye level to me. I've seen him naked numerous times before. But this is different. This time I'm going to have to touch it. It's going inside my body. And that thought is terrifying. Because his cock is larger than any man's I've seen before. Not just long, but thick and fat.

I know how much stretch it will take to get him inside, and I'm not sure I'll ever be able to fit all of him. Enzo isn't the kind of man to wait for me to adjust to his size.

"Stop thinking; this is your punishment. Don't think except what I tell you to think," he commands.

I don't know how he expects me to shut off my mind, but I try. I moisten my lips as I stare longingly at him. Because a man who has a cock like that surely knows how to work it.

Don't think, just trust. Trust my instincts that even though it will be punishment, it will also heal me. Enzo won't hurt me more than I deserve.

"Suck me, Kai."

Suck him. I sucked too many cocks on that yacht. *I hate sucking cock.*

Images of cocks on that yacht start flooding my brain, but I push them out.

"Suck. My. Cock." Enzo's voice brings me back to reality.

I reach forward to grab his cock with my hand, but Enzo's eyes stop me. Instead, I move forward, my mouth parted as my lips brush against the head of his cock.

The heat from it immediately warms my cold shell that has hardened since Enzo grabbed me by the neck.

I let the heat consume me, and Enzo watches me patiently like he's going to allow me as much time as I need to adjust.

But then he thrusts, and his cock is deep within my throat.

I gag at the intrusion, my eyes immediately water. *Fuck him.*

He grabs my chin as my mouth is filled with him.

"Beautiful tears," he says.

He pulls his cock back out.

"Fuck you!" I shout, already losing my cool. *Why did I think this punishment was a good idea? I will hate him when we are finished.*

He grins. "Taking responsibility for your actions is never easy, Kai."

I wipe the tears from my face. "You like me in pain. You're sick!"

He fists my hair, jerking my head back. "No, I don't enjoy your pain. I enjoy the control. I enjoy knowing you are *mine*. I enjoy watching you pay me back with your tears, but I don't enjoy your pain."

His cock pushes at my mouth again, and this time I let

him in easily. I prepare myself for his cock to invade my throat again, but this time he takes his time, pumping into me.

And when his head rolls back, and he moans, I feel the flood of liquid building at my core. I've never seen a man so hot and bothered from the touch of my lips.

So I get bolder with my strokes. I lick over his length, meeting his thrusts and allowing more of his cock into my mouth, until he's hitting the back of my throat again.

The tears still come, but this time I give them willingly. I give them for Zeke—for the pain I caused Enzo. I give them because I want to see Enzo feeling excited. I love the heated desire grow deeper in his eyes with each thrust and knowing I'm the one putting it there.

My panties are soaked as I continue to suck his glorious cock. A cock I already love and want more of. I never knew sucking a man off could bring me pleasure, but it does.

I could spend my life on my knees tasting the tiny beads of his pre-cum. The heat of his blood as his cock grows larger. The thick muscles as it parts my lips.

I want more.

I can't get enough of his cock. The deeper he goes in my throat, the more he moans, the more sensitive my bud grows between my legs, aching to feel more.

Enzo gives me a look, and I know he's about to explode. The look gives me a choice. I can choose where he comes.

I want all of his cum.

So I pull him deeper into my throat, until he's exploding his hot thick cum coating my throat.

He pulls back and stares at me suspiciously.

"You're tougher than I thought."

I smile as I lick my lips, loving the salty taste in my mouth.

"I've had a lot of practice." That was anything but punishment for me.

His body hardens at my comment. I see his hands fist and the thick vein in his neck pops. He hates that any other man has ever touched me. He hates that he sees me as damaged goods.

"Stop looking at me like that," I say.

"Like what?"

"Like I'm damaged. I'm not. Finish your punishment."

"That was the easy part," he warns. And I have no doubt he means it.

I nod, preparing my body for more invasion.

"Strip," he commands.

I've been naked in front of this man before, but it was never leading anywhere. This time it is, and I'm terrified of what he will think of my body.

He raises an eyebrow while he waits for me. He tucks himself back into his jeans but doesn't do them back up. He wants the inequality between us. He'll be clothed, while I'll be naked.

I grab the hem of my shirt and lift it over my head. My nipples instantly point in his direction. I didn't wear a bra, and right now I regret that I don't have another layer of protection between him and me.

He exhales at my naked chest, and I see the appreciation in his eyes instead of the disgust he should feel at my scars. It gives me the courage to remove my jeans and underwear until I'm naked in front of him.

Enzo was angry and mad at what I did when we first entered this room, but now that he remembers what I've been through, I can see his anger dissipate.

"Don't—don't feel sorry for me. Punish me; I deserve it."

He growls.

"You're right. You do."

I walk toward him and grab the waistband of his jeans to strip him, but his hand grabs my wrist and stops me.

"No, down on the floor on all fours."

My eyes widen. *Is he really going to take me the first time while I'm on all fours like an animal?* I won't even be able to look him in the eyes.

I reluctantly get down on my hands and knees, my ass in the air. *What have I gotten myself into?*

I feel his warm hand at my ass as he kneels next to me. *This is it. The moment my life changes again.*

I close my eyes, preparing for the intrusion. I'm wet from sucking him, but I'm not sure it's enough to ease the pain I know is coming.

I jerk forward, but not from his cock entering me, but from his hand meeting the flesh of my ass.

I don't make a sound. I'm used to holding in any signs of pain. I know Jarod used to get hard at any sign of distress he knew he caused me, and I won't let Enzo get the same pleasure.

"You're so used to pain, aren't you? You don't even react to the sting."

He swats my ass again, this time the sting spreads, and I can't help but let my eyes water. I could stop the feeling of the pain. I know how. Just lock myself away. *But do I want to?*

My body starts the process automatically. Stilling, cooling, locking away my mind. My mind goes to the beach, to the sand, to the warm wind.

"Don't you dare," Enzo curses.

His voice breaks through, but it's not enough.

He slaps my ass again, but I can barely feel it.

He flips me over abruptly, until I'm on my back. "You have to feel everything." He spreads my legs open, and his mouth disappears between my legs. At first, I don't know what he is doing. But then, I feel the warmth returning to my body. The heat spreads from his lips to my core. And then I feel the most pleasurable thing I've ever felt—his tongue on my clit.

I've never felt such pleasure before. Never felt such ecstasy. I didn't know how it would feel, but now I never want him to stop.

I arch my back into him, and my toes curl as he licks and sucks over my sensitive bud.

Jesus.

My body comes back to life from his touch. And if sex means I get to experience even a drop of this pleasure, I will never shut down during it again.

"Yes," I moan, grabbing his thick hair holding his head between my legs.

I feel myself building to a place I haven't experienced since he made me come on his bed.

"Yes, fuck yes, Enzo," I curse.

He stops.

He fucking stops.

He grins down on me. "There you are."

"Why did you stop?"

He smirks, wiping my juices from his mouth with his hand. "Because I haven't finished punishing you yet."

I swallow hard, forcing the fear down.

"I will hit you three more times. And you will stay with me for all of them. You will let the tears fall, the cries escape, the moans fill this room. Whatever you feel, you will feel it. You won't lock yourself away—not until you've taken all three."

I nod.

"Do you agree?" he asks needing verbal confirmation.

"Yes."

He grabs my hips and flips my body onto his lap, my ass in the air.

He rubs it gently, and then I still as he presses a finger at my asshole.

I can feel his grin at my body's response. "I should fuck your ass without preparing you, to punish you, but I'm not that cruel. Someday though, this ass will be mine."

Someday? This ends after tonight. This is the only time we get.

"One," Enzo says, slapping my ass harder than before.

I force myself to feel it because it's the only way I might get to the pleasure that comes afterward. And I'm tired of not feeling, even the bad.

My eyes water, but they don't spill.

"Good girl," he says, soothing my ass with his touch.

"Two," he says, striking harder.

I cry out, my tears falling now. My ass is far too sensitive for another. I consider pleading for him to stop, but I don't. I've never felt so alive.

"Three," I brace myself, but it's not enough. This one holds all his rage. All the pain he's feeling inside he takes out in one stroke.

"Fuck," I cry. My tears are full on streams now, my ass burning, my body convulsing.

"It's over, baby."

"Don't, baby me," I cry, pulling my body off his lap. I hate him, but I also want him. I've never been so wet before. I want his cock even though I know it will hurt worse than his slaps. But I am also already tired of feeling—anything, pleasure or pain.

He watches me carefully as he pulls the T-shirt from his

head. Then lowers his jeans and kicks them off until he's naked.

"On the bed," he commands.

"No."

I cross my arms over my chest. I don't want him to fuck me on the bed where he's comfortable. If he takes me, he takes me on the floor.

"It wasn't a question. It was a command."

"No."

"Would you rather take the whipping?"

I feel the redness of my ass. I would need to shut down completely to take a whipping. And Enzo wouldn't let me. It would last days, neither of us relenting until I felt everything.

"On. The. Bed. Kai."

I reluctantly lay down on the bed as he walks toward me. But then I remember my own plan for revenge. It's better this way. And as much as he's hurt me so far, I also feel free. I know he's holding back. If he truly wanted to hurt me, he would. His hits were nothing like Jarod's. Enzo's hits were that of a man in pain expressing his emotion to me in the only way he knows how, because words aren't enough to feel his pain.

And I feel pain too. Pain of what I've been through for six years because of this man. Pain at knowing men died because of me. Pain at not being free.

But that ends now. When Enzo's cock enters me, I will give him all of my pain. I will be free. My pain will be his burden to bear.

He takes a rope and a condom out of his nightstand. He tosses the condom aside and then takes the rope.

My eyes widen. I don't want to be tied down. I won't be able to stop him if I can't handle this. I won't be able to feel his body as he enters me. I've noticed I do better when I initiate the touch first. He's noticed that and is taking it away from me.

"Wrists," Enzo says, waiting patiently by the head of the bed.

I close my eyes, letting the fear overtake me.

"Wrists, baby."

Why is it when he says 'baby' it both calms me and petrifies me at the same time? He wants to hurt me, but he also wants to please me. He can't have it both ways. He can't be the monster and the lover. He has to choose.

And I already know which he will choose. Monster. No lover would tie me up knowing my history.

I raise my hands over my head, and he ties them together and then to the bed frame.

I pull, but there is no way I'll ever get free.

Then, he takes a blindfold from the dresser and covers my eyes.

Shit.

I don't even get to see him.

I get to live in the darkness where I've always wanted, but the darkness is no longer my friend. I feel alone.

I hear the crinkle of the condom as he sheaths himself before settling between my spread legs.

He doesn't kiss me.

Doesn't suck or caress me.

He does nothing to prepare me for his cock.

This is punishment. It's meant to hurt and remind me I don't deserve anything better. He's giving me his pain, and in return, I'll give him mine.

"I hope Langston did fuck you and stretched you out first, because this is going to hurt. And I won't let you lock yourself away again. You will feel this. *All of it.* And you will never hurt my family again."

Anger rages inside—sex should never be a punishment. But this is what I wanted. This is how I get free. By showing Enzo he's a monster no more worthy of becoming Black than I am. He's not a saint who just protects his men and those weaker than him. He's a monster. And until he makes amends for what he did to me, and who knows how many other innocent people before me, he doesn't get to think of himself as anything but evil.

I want to tell him I didn't fuck Langston. But it might give him the resolve he needs to stop himself. And I need him to lose control to do this. I need this.

He needs this.

This ends now.

I almost feel the regret oozing off of him into the room. "I'm just warning you. Even the most experienced women I've been with feel pain at my size. This is your last chance. I won't fuck you unless you want me to. But this will not be gentle. I will not give you time to adjust. This will ruin you if you aren't prepared."

His cock rests at my entrance, and I know the pain I'm about to experience.

I will never be ready for this.

But I want to ruin Enzo as badly as he wants to ruin me.

I need this.

I want this.

This first time is going to hurt no matter what. I'd rather feel all of Enzo than slowly face the reality of him. I want to know the worst, so I'm no longer afraid of sex.

I grab his thick thighs with my legs, pulling him to me. "Do it."

My eyes slip below the blindfold, and I watch as he

closes his eyes as if to prepare himself. When he opens, I see a look of lust I've never seen before. It's like he released all of his self-control.

He gives me one look of warning knowing I can see beneath the blindfold, and then he plunges inside me.

I cry out, releasing all of my fury and pain as he enters me. His burning heat mixes with my ice cold and causes a hurricane of emotion and feelings inside me.

Tears burn my eyes; my thighs squeeze at his waist, and my voice screams out feeling every bit of him stretching inside me.

I feel myself struggling to breathe. Like him being inside me pushed all my air out.

I can do this; breathe.

I look up at Enzo. His eyes are dark holes as he looks at me. He doesn't give me any words to comfort me—nothing to help my struggle. His lust seems to grow the more I struggle beneath him.

I've never felt so alone.

He inches forward, and that's when I realize my body hasn't accepted all of him. There is still more to go. I struggle against the ropes.

I can't.

But Enzo doesn't give me time to prepare or argue against it. He thinks this is what I experienced on a daily basis on that yacht. That I felt worse than this. That this is nothing in comparison. He thinks the reason I'm in pain is because I'm back there again.

It's not.

The pain is real.

The pain at never thinking a man would ever want to fuck me.

That a man would never find me attractive.

That a man would never see me as anything but broken.

Enzo doesn't see me that way. He sees me as a woman deserving to be punished—a woman he is desperate to fuck.

He thrusts again.

"Fuck you," I scream at the pain.

Although Enzo thinks I'm screaming at him.

Another thrust, hitting me so deeply I can't imagine he can go deeper inside.

His hands are at my hips, sinking inside me deeper and deeper. Stretching me wider than I've ever been stretched.

I feel the blood oozing as he penetrates me. I feel myself being ripped.

I feel the tears dripping down my cheeks. But not from the torture—from the release of the pain and agony.

Enzo is setting me free whether he means to or not. This is what my body needs—not a sweet entry into woman-hood. *This.*

I start relaxing, opening myself to the pain as he starts pounding into me in a brutal rhythm meant to torture me with his cock.

But then he changes his angle, and I feel his body rubbing against my clit. The alternating pain and pleasure overwhelm me. Almost forgetting my part I need to release to fully be free. The part he needs to hear.

It takes everything inside me to speak and not in a curse. "I've never been sold."

He stares at me but doesn't slow his thrusts as if he can barely understand what I'm saying.

"I've never been sold. Truth or lie?" I ask.

"You want to play now?"

"Just answer me," I grit out between painful tears.

"Lie."

I nod. But he pounds faster, and the pain turns to quick panting on the verge of coming, but it doesn't make up for the pain he put me through in his journey to get punishment.

"I've never been tortured."

The scars of my torture mark my body, making it an obvious lie.

"Lie."

Faster he pounds into me—rougher, harder. Not relenting, despite my frantic breathing.

It's too much and not enough at the same time.

I hate it and love it.

He hurt me and healed me.

But I will never let him know how much this healed me. He will only ever know of the pain. He will see himself as a monster. When he looks in the mirror, he will only see the boy his father raised him to be—a beast.

I swallow hard, preparing for my next words.

"I've never been raped."

He doesn't hesitate. He thrusts faster, building us both to the edge of everything—pain, joy, forgiveness.

I feel his cock drive into me over and over.

I bite my lip, but it's not enough. I cry out over and over, but I don't know if it's from pain or ecstasy. It all blends together into one mess of emotions.

It is everything.

Everything I've wanted and hated.

I could love this boy, if only he'd let me. Instead, I hate him.

I hate him for selling me.

I hate him for taking me.

I hate him for telling me the truth.

I hate him for punishing me.

I hate him for hurting me.

But I could love him for healing me.

Which is why I'll never think of this moment again. He broke what was left of me, but somehow the final breaking gives me something back. The ability to finally put the pieces back together.

I scream. It's the loudest I've ever screamed. And everything I'm feeling released in one mighty orgasm as I feel Enzo's own release inside as he jerks within my body.

But when he stills, he doesn't relax like a man who just made a woman come. He was so consumed with his own orgasm and revenge, he barely paid attention to me at the end.

We both pant heavily, his cock still rests inside me, and finally, he answers my last truth or lie.

"Lie," he says more cautiously than the rest. "You were raped by Jarod. Langston..." He can't finish his sentence. Still not sure if Langston fucked me or not.

"I've never been raped, and Langston never fucked me. You just took my virginity—ripped it from my body in your seek for revenge. You may not have raped me, but you hurt me instead of loved me. Because you are a monster." And then I say the words I suspect will hurt the worst, "You're just like your father."

I see the crushing pain on his face, and I know I fulfilled my promise. Enzo punished me, but I got my own revenge.

16

ENZO

THAT WAS HER FIRST TIME.

She's never been fucked before.

Never been raped.

Jarod never touched her in that way.

Langston sure as hell didn't.

That's what she's saying. And I can't think of any reason that she'd lie.

Plus, now that I've regained some of my self-control I can see the evidence for myself.

Blood is stained between her legs from where my cock tore away her innocence, her pussy was far too tight, and the tears that rolled down her face as she cursed and writhed in pain is enough to convince me.

She was a virgin—until I ruined her.

I punished her harder than I ever realized because she never told me the truth of what happened to her on that yacht with Jarod.

I assumed he and the other men aboard raped her, but now I know it's not true. *What the hell happened on that boat?* Whatever it was, it hurt her so badly she may never recover.

And I just made it so much worse.

I feel a torrent of guilt for my actions—instant regret.

This should have been the opposite of her first time. This was far too violent for anyone's first time. Far too brutal for most people's ever times.

I shouldn't have used sex to punish her. But I also knew I would struggle whipping her, beating her, scarring her. Not when I could see the physical scars all over her body the entire time I was doing it.

And then she goaded me. *She wanted this.*

Why?

So I would feel the same pain she does now.

I feel like a monster.

This is something my father would do—ruin a woman's first time.

There is no way Kai will ever let me fuck her again. I doubt she will let any man touch her for years, possibly ever.

And it's my fault.

I hurt her—when I promised her I never would.

At least, not in this way.

I'm a monster.

I brought the torture she must have only dreamed about to life.

Did she even come?

I was so consumed by my own feelings—revenge, punishment, and euphoria, that it all went by in a blur.

From the tears streaming down her rosy red cheeks, I'm not sure any of it was enjoyable for her.

"Baby—" I start, but she immediately cuts me off.

"I don't want to hear your apology any more than you want to hear mine. There is nothing to apologize for anyway. I wanted this. I planned this. I wanted you to ruin me; it was the price I was willing to pay. I was already broken anyway."

"Kai," I try again.

By now she's sniffling hard, trying to suck the tears back into her body.

Did she tell me to stop?

I try to think back; I don't remember her telling me to stop. This wasn't rape, but it wasn't good. Even if she wasn't a virgin, it wasn't good.

I hurt her, and I didn't care.

But I won't apologize for what I did.

She needed to be punished, and this was the punishment she chose.

My cock still rests inside her. And I can feel her muscles tightening gently around me. Her pussy is so tight; I don't know how she's tolerating me still buried between her muscles.

I try a different route. "You win."

She blinks rapidly, trying to expel the tears from her eyes, since she can't use her hands currently tied above her head.

"You win. I surrender. You were right; I feel disgusting. I shouldn't, but I do. This was two consensual adults having sex, but I still feel gross, wrong, sick. It's too easy to compare myself to what my father did."

"What did your father do?"

I hesitate, "Zeke didn't tell you?"

"No, I just guessed. If the myths were true about Black, your father must have been one evil guy. I'm sure he tried to pass that along to you. And I see your daily struggle to manage both sides of yourself. The good and the bad."

"There is no good."

She doesn't respond, but I know that was part of her

gaining power here, to make me feel like I'm only evil. Only the bad part of myself controls my actions. It gives her more power if she can predict if she's dealing with the good or bad version of me.

"What happened?" she asks.

I shake my head. She hasn't earned that story. She doesn't get to know why my father was the evilest bastard ever to walk this earth.

She sighs, and her eyes glance down to my cock still inside her. I'm not as hard as I was before, but fucking her once wasn't enough. Her tightness keeps me hard the entire time; I just need to persuade her to try another round. One where I ensure she comes and it feels good.

Because now that I've had her, I don't ever want to stop. She's the most responsive woman I've ever been with. I've never felt a cunt grab hold of me like hers did. And the screams that leave her throat make me possessive and mad. I want her—all of her. The spitfire, the beauty, the fearlessness. Not once was she afraid, no matter the pain I put her through. She took everything.

And as much as she can try to convince me that I've ruined her, other than the tears, she doesn't look hurt. She has a glow about her, which again, might be the tears, but I don't think so. She's radiant, her cheeks have pinked, and her eyes read more confidence and determination in them than I've ever seen.

This changed her.

For worse.

For better.

And I want to know why. Only then will I decide what to do next. Make amends by fucking her, or release her and return to being enemies.

"Tell me what happened on that yacht," I command.

She frowns. "Untie me and get your cock out of me first."

"No."

She glares. "Enzo, untie me. My story is too vulnerable for me to tell when I have no control."

"I think this is the exact position you need to tell me in."

We return stares, neither of us giving in. We are both stubborn, but she forgets that right now, I have all the power. Because she's the one tied to my bed.

"You hurt me; the least you could do is untie me."

"We both hurt each other. I might be the latest person to start the war, but I'm offering an olive branch as soon as I find out the truth."

She takes a deep breath, her back arching and her wrists pulling as if trying one more time to break free. And when it doesn't work, she starts her story.

"When I was first sold, I thought that was all they wanted. I knew the high price they paid for me. I was branded a virgin on that stand when I was sold. It got them a higher price because of it. I knew what my purpose would be when I was taken aboard that yacht.

"But then, the first night, it didn't happen. I was attacked. Men ripped my clothes from my body. They beat me. Whipped me. Forced their cocks down my throat. Did their best to wrench tears from my eyes. But they never came."

She closes her eyes, and I know she's back on that boat.

I rock into her pussy as gently as I can, trying to bring her back to me and away from that horrible place. I watch her nipples peak, and her pussy lips tighten around my cock the tiniest bit, confirming she's still with me. She opens her eyes again.

"That became their game. Their favorite way to torture

me. With promises of what tomorrow would bring. Tomorrow they would rape me. That promise came every day for a month, until slowly I stopped believing the threats. I thought I was safe, at least for the moment. I thought they were saving me for another man who had yet to board the yacht. At one point, I thought you had directed them not to touch me."

I shake my head no.

"But then, they started taking other women on board." She winces as she relives it.

"Kai, come back to me."

Her eyes flutter back to mine immediately. "They would rape those women as soon as their feet touched the deck—always in front of me. They would torture me while I watched them violate other women, while I was hopeless to save them.

"The men made me feel like I was disgusting, unworthy, less than. That I wasn't pretty enough for any man to rape or touch."

Her eyes are completely filled with tears, but she doesn't let them fall—not now. She's too strong to let them out.

"But then, my body took over. I had to cope, and in my sick mind, I started wishing they would rape me. I wanted off that boat, and the women who were raped got to leave, usually in body bags, but it didn't matter, it was an end. But it wasn't just that. The thought of being raped seemed easier than the torture I went through.

"Eventually, my brain filled in the dots with other women's rapes. I pretended their rapes were mine until I couldn't even tell I was lying to myself. That was their plan: to torture my brain. Make me believe things were worse than they were. My imagination was worse than anything they could have actually done to me."

"Kai," I say, my heart breaking for her.

"They say there are worse things in life than death. I believe that. What they did to me messed with my head. It's why I can't tolerate anyone's touch. Because the only time they touched me was to beat me. I never got comfort—nothing that could be misperceived as caring. I didn't even get a sexual release. I got nothing. I was nothing but a punching bag that they tormented until my mind broke and I could no longer determine what was real and what was fake."

"I'm sor—"

"Don't. You don't get to be sorry for what I went through. You don't get to be sorry for anything you did. You were the catalyst. You started this. If we went back to that yacht that day with your hands around my throat, I would have chosen death knowing what came next."

"You said no one could touch you, but I touched you."

She stares at me, lips parted, with no explanation as to why.

"You hugged Langston and comforted Zeke even though you were in pain. In time, you will be able to touch anyone you want without the spark of pain. But for now, you have me."

She chuckles. "You just tortured me into submission. You punished me. My body will no longer respond to you the same way."

"That may have been your intention. You may have hoped to make us permanent enemies with this stunt. You may have thought this would ensure we would never forgive each other and squash any connection we had. That from now on, we would be nothing but enemies ready to fight. But that didn't happen, did it?"

She gasps. "What do you mean?"

"I mean, if you really wanted my cock out, you would have pushed me out long ago. That if you were really so hurt, you would be flinching in pain any time I touch you."

I grab her hips and rock forward.

Her eyes glaze over, part from the pain, but also from something else.

"Did you come?" I ask.

She freezes.

"Did. You. Come?"

"That question isn't relevant. Lots of women come from sexual experiences they don't enjoy."

I flare my nostrils and growl low and heavy. "That means yes, you came."

She looks at me like she's going to kill me for telling the honest truth.

I smirk, *damn I'm good.* Even when I punish a woman, I'm still the best she ever had. I guess in Kai's case I'm also the worst. Because I'm the only man she's ever had.

"Don't get cocky. It had nothing to do with you," she says.

"Sure it didn't. But just to prove you wrong, how about I make you come again?"

"Enzo," Kai warns.

I rock my hardening cock, and her juices instantly soak me.

I move slow, letting her decide what she wants.

"You want me—don't deny it. You've had it rough, punishing because deep down that's what Jarod made you think you deserve. It's what your body convinced you was all you could handle. But it's not the truth. The truth is, everything about sex can be magical with the right partner," I say.

Her lips part, and her tongue licks her bottom lip in anticipation.

I have her. Now just close the deal.

"For instance," I jerk my hips forward until I rub against her sensitive clit, and the angle of my cock presses deep within her most likely hitting her G-spot. "When a man knows how to read your body, it can be the most explosive thing you've ever experienced."

I gyrate my hips, making small circles over her clit and within her cunt. Her legs spread wider for me, and a small whimper escapes her lips.

She has to be sore and in pain, but that's not what I want her thinking about when his ends.

I want her to remember the explosive feeling when she comes around my cock. How I was the only man to ever make her feel that way. And how she only wants me to be the one to give it to her again.

She's mine.

And I don't want her to forget that—ever.

Even when we have long finished our time together, I want her to think back to her first and know that no man will ever bring her the same amount of pleasure as me.

"Let me show you how good it can feel."

She throws her head back as I thrust harder and grip her hips, forcing all of my length inside her.

"Is that a yes?"

She moans as I lean down and take a nipple into my mouth, sucking viciously.

"Kai? If I don't get a yes, then I'll stop. What will it be?"

I've teased her, given her every opportunity to know what it will be like now if she lets me fuck her. Now, it's up to her.

"Yes."

Thank God!

Last time was about punishment. This time, it will be nothing but pleasure.

But it doesn't mean I will fuck her gently. Our connection is too passionate for anything gentle. The crash of sparks at a simple touch will ensure anytime we fuck it will be epic.

I lean down and remove the blindfold that had already started falling from her face as I thrust in and out of her slickness.

I lean down and kiss her, like she's the only woman I ever want to kiss. And from the taste of her, it might be true.

Her tongue pushes back, driving into me with a dance showing that even though she wants this, she won't give up power completely to me.

I push her legs back toward her head as I pump into her, allowing a deeper angle to hit all of her depths.

"Fuck..." she moans, and water burns her eyes again.

"Too much?" I ask. *Please don't let it be too much.* I can barely stand to go as carefully as I'm going.

"No, don't you dare stop. It shouldn't feel good, but it does."

I halt, grabbing her chin and looking deep into her sea green eyes. "Don't ever say sex shouldn't feel good. You were turned on when you sucked my cock. You were wet when I spanked your ass. Drenched from being tied up. You wanted this. You enjoyed this, and there is nothing wrong with you. Plenty of women like the unordinary—the dark, the dangerous. You can like this. You can like plain missionary. You can like getting fucked in the ass. Or tied up. Or on top. Or in any position you want with any person you want, male or female. Don't let Jarod take that from you. This— this is right. If it feels good; it's right."

"This feels good," she says with a tiny smile.

"Now, what do you want, baby? Tell me what you want, and it's yours."

She blushes.

"Fuck me hard, fast, and painful—like before. I don't care about the pain; it just made the release all the sweeter when I finally came."

She came. Even though it hurt at first, her first time was still pleasurable. That makes the sinking feeling inside shrink just a little. I'm not completely like my father.

I smile.

"My pleasure."

I push her legs back again as I drive into her with all my force.

She cries out, but this time I listen closely. It hurts her, but it also releases her from the pain of before.

But I want more pleasure than pain for her this time. So I let my thumb find her nub and press against it in tiny circles while I fuck her deeper and deeper.

Her arms pull at the rope, and her body writhes beneath me.

"God, it's all so much. I never knew..."

"You never knew what?"

"It could feel like this." She cries out again as I hit the deeper depths still.

I cradle her head in my hands as I kiss her in rhythm with my thrusts.

I've already come twice, and I'm about to come a third time, far quicker than I want to. But I'm determined not to come until Kai has.

"Come, baby. Let go."

I'm not sure she'll listen to me. She rarely does. But her

pretty eyelashes flutter in my direction, her lips part, and her body contracts.

"Damn you, Enzo!" she screams out as her pussy convulses around me, releasing her orgasm in an explosion. Her cry loud enough that I'm sure any visitors outside could hear her.

Her cries are my cue, and I pump one more time, releasing my load into her core before collapsing on top of her body.

For the first time in forever, I feel whole lying on top of her with my cock still buried inside her.

"Enzo?" comes Kai's sweet voice.

"Yes?"

"As much as I enjoy coming, I don't think my pussy can handle any more stretching for today. And my arms would love blood circulation to return to them," she snarks.

I smile.

"Ready?" I ask.

She narrows her eyes, clearly not understanding my meaning. So I go with the ripping the bandaid off method.

I pull out in one stroke, my cock still thick from being inside her.

She winces, blowing out a hiss as I pull myself from her body.

Only then do I see how much she bled and the damage I truly did to her.

She was a virgin—but now she's not.

I remember my first time. I was fifteen, and the woman was a stripper at Surrender. I think eighteen or nineteen. It was expected of me, so I did. It wasn't life-changing.

But this was for Kai.

I pull the condom off that carried two of my loads. I'm

not sure how protective using the same condom twice is. Probably not one of my best ideas.

"Let me clean you up," I say, carrying the condom to dispose of.

"No."

For once, I disobey her no. I run to the bathroom, grab a washcloth and then return to between her legs to wipe as much of the blood as I can.

She winces, but I doubt it's from the pain. More from me taking care of her. She feels weak, and she hates feeling weak.

"Thanks," she says when I stop.

I should release her arms, but this is the last moment of complete control I have. So I take advantage of it.

"I'm—"

"Don't you dare say you are sorry."

I cover her mouth with my hand so she can't talk.

"I'm not sorry. Not at all. At least, not for tonight. Because without the excuse of punishment, you would have never let me fuck you. And as painful as it was, it also healed you. I see it in your eyes. When we first met, I was seventeen and you were sixteen, I wanted to be your first. But once you were sold, I knew it would never be possible. You may think you stole something from me, and you did steal power and forced me to face my own evil that lives inside me, but I also got a gift I never thought I'd have. I got the gift of showing you how incredible sex can be."

She tries to speak, but I keep her mouth closed.

"So thank you. Thank you for trusting me with your first time, even if it was meant to hurt me. It did. But it also was the best fucking time I've ever had."

Slowly, I release her mouth, and she stares with her lips

parted, her hair a tangled mess on top of her head. I begin to undo the ropes before she speaks.

"You can be a monster, and I did want to hurt you. And I did, if only for a moment. But I did trust you with my first time."

I smile.

"But don't let it get to your head. I trusted you with my first time, because you are the only man who doesn't cause me to flinch every time he touches me."

I laugh. "I'll have plenty more times to show you just how incredible it can be."

She goes silent.

I finally release the ropes from her wrists.

And then an awkward silence falls between us. Neither of us knows what to say.

"I'm going to run you a bath. It will help with the soreness that is coming."

She nods.

I start the bath and then return. She's sitting on the edge of the bed with a blank stare and soft smile on her lips.

"The bath is ready."

I want to scoop her up, but I know her well enough to know that's not what she wants. It's one of the reasons she didn't tell me until it was too late she was a virgin. She didn't want to be treated differently. She wanted to be treated like an equal.

But when she gets to the tub, I can't help but hold my hand out to help her into the tub.

She takes my hand and then sinks down her chin, her eyes close, and she whimpers softly at the warm water.

I smile as I kneel next to the tub.

"You aren't coming in?"

"If I come in, you'll only end up even more sore, which defeats the purpose of the bath."

Her eyes widen, but she doesn't say anything.

What's going on in that head of yours?

A knock startles me.

Kai and I exchange glances, but dread fills me. It could be Langston or the doctor coming to say Zeke took a turn for the worse.

"Be right back," I tell Kai.

I grab a pair of boxers to put on before I answer the bedroom door.

Archard is standing in the doorway, looking concerned.

"Is Zeke okay?" I ask.

"He's fine. Making jokes and hitting on the nurses. I think he'll make a full recovery."

I exhale the breath I was holding and smile. It sounds like Zeke.

"What do you need then, Archard?"

"Is Miss Miller here?"

"Yes, but she's taking a bath."

"I need to speak to both of you."

I frown. I don't like him coming anywhere near her when she's naked. But the bubbles were covering her the last time I saw her, and from Archard's look, this seems important.

I nod for him to follow me. I notice the bloodied sheets on my bed that look like a massacre happened instead of sex.

I smile, I would love to see his face when he noticed the blood. Instead, I hurry into the bathroom first to check that Kai is covered. She is. I give her a look of warning before Archard enters.

Kai tenses when she sees him, but not because she's

naked. She has no problem with her nakedness. But because we both know why Archard would want to talk to us together.

"The first event is ready. This is your twenty-four-hour notice. The first task was chosen by Mr. Miller. But that's the only clue I can give you. Meet me at Surrender at nine AM tomorrow."

I glance at the clock realizing it's nine AM in the morning. It's been a long night. And our lives are about to get harder. I may have fucked Kai. She may have served her punishment, and so did I. We may have even started a path toward forgiveness. But whatever our relationship is, it's new. And before we have a chance to explore what sexual connection we could have, we are going to be forced into being enemies. And I doubt after tomorrow we can continue to be both—lovers and enemies. We can only be one. And our only choice is to remain enemies.

17

KAI

IT WAS SUPPOSED to feel like punishment.

The sex was supposed to make him feel regret and pain.

Instead, it brought us closer into a connection I still don't understand.

It was meant to be only one time. Hurt him and heal myself—that's all.

But then I let him fuck me again.

And his words promised another fuck later if I'm willing.

That wasn't supposed to happen.

Enzo wasn't supposed to care for me after he fucked me.

He was supposed to hurt me and make me hate him even more.

Instead, it's hard to look at him as anything but my protector. But tomorrow no matter what he wants, that ends. He can't protect me and beat me.

The games start tomorrow.

Everything up to this point has been playtime.

Now it's serious.

I have twenty-four-hours to prepare for a battle I don't even know.

And right now, I'm sore as fuck.

Enzo's cock was far larger than anything I could ever imagine. He stayed in me for far too long. And stretched me to my limit. But it felt so damn good.

I will never tell him that though. His ego is already too big.

I can't stay in this tub all day, as much as I want to. And when I get out, I can't snuggle with Enzo in his oversized bed like I want to either. I'm not sure he would want to anyway. That's not how we are together.

Archard left us after giving us our warning. Not that his warning is much help. *How do you prepare for a battle where you don't know what weapon will be used? Or how the battle will be fought?*

You can't.

I try to think about what tasks my father might assign to try to give me an advantage. But when he wrote the rules, I was just a baby. He didn't know he'd never have a son. He didn't know that I would be fighting. And he did nothing to prepare me anyway.

I'm destined to lose. And after how I handled the last crisis, getting men killed, and a high-level leader almost killed, it's probably for the best that I don't stand a chance.

"Baby, what are you thinking?"

"That you should stop calling me 'baby' and start thinking of me as the enemy."

Enzo's eyes drop, and he gives me a chilling look.

You don't get to be my friend. You don't get to be my lover. You are my enemy.

Why can't you see that?

This was supposed to cement our hate for each other, not make us want each other more.

"Can you hand me a towel?" I ask.

"Sure."

Enzo grabs a towel and holds it open while I climb out of the tub before wrapping it around my body.

He sold you, don't ever forget that.

Don't fall for the charming grin and seductive eyes.

Forget how good he made your body feel.

Enzo doesn't move out of my way. We stand—both in various states of nakedness, but it's not just our bodies exposed to each other, but our souls.

"I'm going to get dressed."

"Okay."

"And then I'm going to prepare for tomorrow."

"Okay," his lips tighten.

"Okay."

Neither of us move. When this moment is over, so are we. I'm sure after tomorrow any feelings we have toward each other will be severed.

Finally, I walk past him, our arms touch and then our fingers brush against each other as if we want to hold onto each other's hands.

We could have made a great couple. The sex is out of this world. We are drawn to each other even when we consider the other person an enemy. But it would have never worked out long term. Just like a flame that eventually dies out quickly with a burst of strong wind. We would have been snuffed out just as quickly.

It's a good thing this can never happen between us. We definitely can't have a relationship, and even fucking each other would bring up too many emotions between us. But it would have been fun to ride his cock while we could, before we let the drama come into our lives.

Too bad it took me until the last possible day to decide it was okay to fuck him.

I walk into the closet and pull on some running shorts, sports bra, and tank top. I'm not in the best of shape and decide I should spend today testing my abilities so tomorrow, no matter what I face, I will at least know what my skills are.

When I come back out, Enzo is dressed in jeans and a charcoal T-shirt.

"Going for a run?" he asks.

"I don't want to stay here—not during the games. I should be staying with my father. He could help me prepare."

"I could help you prepare."

I snort. "Yea, you could. And then you would know exactly what my weaknesses and strengths are."

His jaw tenses. "You aren't leaving."

"Let me leave for today. You can send one of your men to monitor me. I just really need to be alone today."

"No."

Enzo turns away, and I know this is a done conversation. He's never going to let me go. He likes controlling me too much.

Damn him.

I don't care if Enzo knows my strengths and weaknesses. He knows mine already, and I already know his. I just need some space after what happened to get my head on straight.

I run downstairs and out onto the sand. The sun is already beating down with plenty of moisture in the air despite a cloudless sky. It's going to be a hot one.

I stretch for a moment, staring at the sea that feels like my enemy.

You will not hurt me.

I take a deep breath, filling my lungs with oxygen, and then I run.

I run as fast as I can for as long as I can on the sand.

I know Enzo's property is vast, much larger than I can imagine. But I intend to run further than the edge of his property line. I know he has dozens of men watching his property. He has cameras and more security than I could imagine.

Enzo can do his best to keep me here, but it doesn't mean I have to stay.

I run, my lungs burning, my legs aching the entire time.

Fuck, I'm weak. Weaker than I've ever been. I've never been much of a runner or exerciser, but working all the time and running from my father's debt collectors kept me fit.

I see Enzo's property line come into view as men patrol the edge with fencing almost all the way to the edge of the beach.

That's my goal.

But five minutes later I lay passed out on the sand, my chest heaving to catch my breath.

Fuck, I'm out of shape.

Hopefully, my father didn't plan anything that involved endurance, because I won't win that fight.

I look at my puny arms. It better not involve strength either.

Fuck, I'm screwed.

It doesn't matter—this all just a formality. Hopefully the tests aren't too dangerous, and I can survive until Enzo wins. Then I can convince him to let me go free.

"What are you doing?" I hear Langston's voice.

"Getting a suntan."

He smiles over me.

I squint as I look up at him, the sun blinding me.

"Decide to go for a run?"

"Yes, although it was more of a crawl. I have no stamina anymore."

He smirks. "That's not what it sounded like last night."

My cheeks redden, and I gasp. "You heard us?"

"I think the entire city heard you."

I laugh. "Sorry."

"Don't worry; I've already scrubbed out my ears."

I nod.

He studies me for a moment, as a thought twists in his head.

"What?" I ask.

"Come with me."

I don't like the swift mood change, but I stand up and follow him. Sweat coats my body, and my legs ache with every step. After the first task I really need to start working out again and at least make an attempt at protecting myself.

We walk back towards the house and around to a private area on the side of the house.

"Zeke!" I say happily. He's sitting in a chair with his feet in the sand.

He smiles back at me.

"You're out of bed. That must mean you're feeling better and out of the woods?" I ask.

He nods. "I'm feeling well enough to help teach you a thing or two."

I cock my head, not understanding. I look from Zeke to Langston, and then I notice what else is new. Two targets planted in the sand.

"What are you talking about?"

"We decided Zeke and I should teach you some of the basics before tomorrow. We can only do so much with the limited time we have, but knowing how to shoot a gun at least could come in handy tomorrow."

My lips curl up. "Does Enzo know about your plans?"

Langston gives Zeke a worried glance.

Damn, I like these two. Enzo may be their boss, and they would follow him to the ends of the earth, but they also make up their own minds and do what they think is best.

"What Enzo doesn't know won't hurt him," Zeke answers.

I grin.

"Here," Langston says handing me a gun he pulls from the back of his pants.

I take the gun, it feels heavy in my hands, but I don't feel dangerous holding it. I doubt even if I knew how to aim, that I would be able to shoot anyone with it—least of all Enzo.

Langston goes over the basic mechanics of how to load the bullets, how to check the safety, and how to aim, with Zeke jumping in occasionally when he has things to add.

And then I'm standing in front of a target with a gun in my hand, rapidly firing the gun. My first few bullets barely hit the edges of the target, but with a quick adjustment, I hit the bullseye almost every time.

"I think you need to back up and try some more, but you are a natural," Zeke says.

"But don't forget, it's easy when no one is firing back. All dangerous men carry a gun, even when they aren't supposed to. Be prepared for them to turn a gun on you at any second," Langston says.

I nod, taking in Langston's words. Then I exhale deeply

as I back up and fire off more shots, hitting the bullseye again and again. It's a thrilling feeling to be holding something so dangerous in my hands and knowing if I aimed it at a person, I could kill them.

Zeke and Langston must really trust me if they feel safe with me holding a gun.

"What are you doing?" Enzo asks, stepping down from the deck as he walks toward us.

We all freeze and stare in Enzo's direction. Even when he's dressed so casually, he holds the power to get a room full of thousands of people to follow his orders with only his voice.

"Teaching her the basics to protect herself," Zeke answers.

Enzo shakes his head as he stops walking a few feet away.

"You aren't protecting her by teaching her how to shoot. You're only giving her false hope that she actually has a chance at winning," Enzo says.

I frown. Any pleasant feelings from earlier disappear with his words. I embody rage, and without thinking I aim the gun in Enzo's direction, but instead of aiming for his heart like Langston taught me, I aim for just off his shoulder.

Enzo looks at me smugly, and I stare back at him.

He doesn't reach for his own gun, even though I know he has one on him. He always does anytime he leaves his bedroom. Langston and Zeke don't try to stop me.

I squeeze the trigger, aiming for a spot on the deck behind him, knowing if I miss and hit him, the worst damage I'll do is to his shoulder. I won't come close to killing him.

As I planned the bullet hits the deck behind Enzo.

The world stops, and I wait for Enzo's retribution.

He smirks. "You missed."

My own smug expression drops from my face. *Enzo wanted me to shoot him.* Maybe I should have, that might make whatever happens tomorrow a more fair fight.

He turns and walks back to the deck, not worried at all I might shoot him in the back.

"Oh, and you might want to teach her how to drive since she can't do that either."

I glare in his direction and consider firing again, but I don't trust myself with a moving target. I could miss and kill him. Which right now wouldn't be such a bad thing. Except then I'd become Black, and I'm not sure I'm ready or willing to take the job.

I don't want to rule an empire. I don't want to spend my days keeping people in line with my gun.

I look out at the ocean. Even if it gives me such beauty and luxury. Giving me a life of ease.

I don't want it. I turn back and see Enzo slip into the house. Especially if it turns me into a grumpy, unfeeling, lonely man like Enzo.

But I can't let his comments go unchecked. I need to feel rage tomorrow; I will need adrenaline pumping through my veins to aid me in my quest. But I don't need all out anger.

Anger will only serve as a distraction.

I start stomping toward the house when Langston calls, "Gun, Kai."

He holds out his hand as if waiting for me to relinquish it to him.

His eyes read serious. He may like me, but he won't let me hurt his boss or closest friend.

I put on the safety, and then toss the gun in his direction. He catches it with ease.

"Thanks for the lessons."

Both men nod.

"But I have other business to attend to." I stomp into the house, intent on giving Enzo a piece of my mind. Because I will not let him win before the games have even started—not anymore.

18

ENZO

Kai's a good shot.

And it pisses me off. Not that she's amazing at everything she does, as I expect her to be, but because no one ever helped her unlock her potential. I don't care that she's a girl, if she had been properly trained she would have been a formidable opponent. But as she is now, I'll destroy her.

For the longest time, I hoped that my opponent would be the stronger one. That it would be clear they were the better man, the one worthy of becoming Black. But then I faced reality. No one would ever be stronger than me; my father ensured that. So I became Black. For three years I've done the job. I lined my pockets with more money. Filled my bed with the sexiest of women. Hired the most dangerous of men.

But I never wanted it. *Any of it.*

And now I don't have a choice. There is no way Kai could win. And even if she could, I can't let her. Only the cruelest of men deserve to be trapped in this life. And I would never wish this life for Kai.

Whether Kai truly wants to become Black or not doesn't

matter. It won't stop her from fighting with everything she has tomorrow. Her father chose the first task. He might have chosen something that plays to her strengths. And I can't let her win—not one round.

I won't let her become Black.

I don't know what I was thinking when I went out there to taunt her. I was angry and pissed that she could stop fucking me so easily. I thought I rocked her world. I know I did, but it wasn't enough.

I should head to Surrender or one of my other bars to pick up a woman for tonight. It would help me blow off steam and be focused for tomorrow. But that thought makes my stomach turn up in disgust.

For the present moment, there is only one woman who would be able to get my cock up. And she almost shot me in the arm.

If she had wanted to, she would have, and I would have deserved it.

I grin.

My fiery woman.

No, not my anything.

She's nothing more than my prisoner and enemy. The only reason I keep her here is to keep track of her. And to protect her—that's it.

The back door opens as I'm standing in the kitchen staring into the fridge, trying to find something light to eat that won't slow me down tomorrow.

"What the hell was that? You've resorted to taunting me now? You really that desperate to win tomorrow?" Kai storms into the kitchen, ready for a fight.

I slam the refrigerator door closed.

Kai crosses her arms, her curvy hips swaying in annoyance.

"Just trying to even the score."

"How so?"

"You ran out this morning like I didn't just fuck your brains out last night. Like that didn't fucking change everything. Like you could live without doing that again."

"I could. I will."

My jaw tenses, my lips thin, and my eyes darken. "No, you couldn't."

She rolls her eyes. "I've lived without sex for twenty-three years. You think I couldn't go another few weeks until this is finished without fucking my enemy?"

"Stop calling me that."

"That's what you are: my enemy. My captor. The asshole who sold me. I can also call you bastard, jerk, dick, fucktwat, motherfucker, son of a bitch. Which would you prefer?"

I smirk. "That's not what you were calling me last night. If I remember correctly you were calling me 'oh God,' and 'yes,' and 'fuck yes.' I prefer one of those names."

She shakes her head slightly. "Just leave me alone. We should both be preparing for whatever awaits us tomorrow. We both need a clear head so we don't get ourselves killed."

"Exactly," I say taking a step into her personal bubble.

Her eyes heat as my own eyes travel up and down her body letting her know exactly what I think of her skimpy workout outfit.

"Not going to happen," she says.

"Don't act like you don't want me in your bed every fucking night."

"I don't."

"We can be enemies during the day and lovers at night."

"No."

"It would help keep us from being distracted during the game."

"I don't see how."

"Because we still have the same chemistry as before. As much as you tried to put a stop to that by your stunt, it didn't change anything. You want me. I want you. We both know this can't go anywhere. We both hate each other anyway. This would never be anything but sex. And when one of us becomes Black, it ends. We go our separate ways."

"You'll release me."

"Yes."

"Good."

"So do we have an arrangement?"

"About the you letting me go part? Yes."

I shake my head and move closer until I all but touch her with my entire body.

She stills, trying to adjust to me being in her space and knowing I could, and will, touch her. She has to decide how far this will go.

"And the fucking?" I ask.

Kai breathes heavily, her eyes going down to stare at the bulge in my jeans. She closes her eyes as if that will help her change her feelings.

She fucking wants me.

She can't deny it.

I can see the way her perky breasts harden with a look from me.

"Go fuck one of your whores at the club," she says, with devastatingly sad and determined eyes.

She's trying to taunt me into hurting her so she won't want to fuck me. *Not going to happen, sweetie.*

"Not when I could have the sexiest, most fucking gorgeous woman with the tightest pussy I've ever felt; and hear the most beautiful voice screaming my name as I torture her with my cock."

She gasps and then bites her lip to silence her mouth in the adorable way she always does right before I get my way with her.

"You can hate me, and still fuck me," I say.

"I will definitely hate you."

"Is that a yes?"

"That's a—you better fuck me like I'm the only woman you ever want, but I'm going to fuck you like each thrust is a dagger into your heart."

She said yes. I don't care how badly she hates me. The hate only makes everything better. Because there is no better way I can think of to spend the rest of the day.

I grab her curvy hips and jerk her body to me. Her soft body slams to my stone core. And my lips hover over hers, but I don't kiss her yet. She may not hate when I touch her like everyone else, but I've learned if she's begging for my touch, it's better than if I take it.

Her cool breath sends shivers down my spine. She doesn't close the gap though, almost enjoying the anticipation as much as I am.

My eyes heat into burning fires of need.

"Kiss me," she says.

I do better. I devour her.

My mouth takes all of her mouth in mine—kissing all of her. My tongue deepens the kiss instantly needing to taste her. I only just had her a few hours ago, but already that was too long ago.

I need this woman in my bed for nights on end to have a chance of extinguishing my desire for her. But it seems she's going to want to argue every time I want to fuck her, rather than just fuck. And if it makes me this excited to argue with her before I fuck her, it will be worth it.

But what if I can't convince her in the future?

What if this is it? Her hatred for me will most likely intensify if I have to betray her or make her look like a fool during the game.

So I'm going to engrain this moment in my head in case it's the last time. I'm used to living that way. In my life, there is no guarantee I will wake up tomorrow. No guarantee I won't have a bullet in my head and end up six feet under.

But with Kai, it's different. I've never felt anything in my life so intense, yet also pleasurable. There has never been a woman like her, and after I become Black again, there will never be one after. I will return to fucking nameless woman I sleep with once, then never see again.

"Why are you such a good fucking kisser?" she asks between kisses.

I give her an evil, seductive look.

She laughs and then angers. "Oh...that was stupid."

"No question is stupid."

"Mine was. It's because you have countless women in your bed every night."

I should comfort her. I know I should, but I like seeing the jealous side. I haven't been with a woman since Kai came back into my life. But I'm not sure I want her to know the whole truth.

I trail my kisses down her neck. She tilts her head to allow me better access. "But you're the only one in my bed," I say.

I kiss her again, and we both shiver. I love touching her icy skin. It twists with my warm and makes me crazy; seeking the feeling I only get when I touch her.

"Let's go get in that bed now," she says; her voice heavy, her eyelids hooded.

"No."

Her lips drop into a frown. "What? I thought—"

"I need you here first." I need her in every part of my house. I need to mark her and make her realize how much she's mine.

She's only ever been mine.

That thought drives me wild. I know her first wasn't as it should have been. I know her head is fucked up from what Jarod did to her. But I love that she's only ever had me.

I'm the only one who can touch her.

Kiss her.

Fuck her.

I've never cared before, but there is something very caveman about wanting a woman to only be yours.

"But Langston and Zeke could walk in. Westcott could—"

I kiss her, trying to shut her up.

"You insufferable man. We are not fucking here."

"Yes, we are. Westcott's job is to be invisible. He knew the second we started talking to leave. And Zeke and Langston got the message loud and clear to not come into the house."

"Did you text them?"

"No, when I marked you as my territory outside."

"I'm am not an object!"

"Doesn't matter. You're mine."

I see the look change in her eyes. From relaxed to hate. And I'm not mad about it at all. Because the lust is still there.

"I hate you."

"I hate you more."

She dives her teeth into my bottom lip until I'm sure she's drawn blood. *Fucking incredible woman.*

No one stands up to me. *Ever.* And if they do, they usually end up dead. But with Kai, I want more. I both love it and hate it when she defies me. I crave it as much as I crave her pussy.

"Strip," I command.

She laughs. "Not going to happen."

I cock my head and smile. My eyes already imaging her without her clothes on. "Tired of strutting around the place naked?" I ask, even though I know it's not about that. She isn't afraid to show her body. She just doesn't like giving up control to me.

"No."

"Prove it."

"You can't goad me."

I kiss her neck again, and a soft moan escapes her lips.

She claws at my neck, and I know I've won, but she won't go down gently.

I grab the hem of her shirt pushing it upward, needing it off her body.

Her eyes dance, and then she grabs my shirt by the neck and rips until it is in two pieces.

"If you wanted me to strip, you just had to ask, baby."

"Don't call me baby."

I jerk her shirt off her head, before she protests again.

"Shorts off, now, baby."

She glares.

"Fine, I'll do it," I say at her silent protest.

I pull her shorts down, hoist her ass up on the counter, and then kneel in front of her.

"What are you doing?"

"Eating you out."

"But I'm sweaty and—fuck."

I taste her sweet juices as I bury my head in her pussy. I'm used to women waxing and going bare, but after having a taste of Kai's pussy, I don't know if I will ever go back. There is something sexy about the way her hair hides the prize from me.

"Jesus effing Christ," she calls out as she grips my hair.

I grip her ass cheeks in my hands, holding her body tightly to my lips. She wiggles in my grasp, my touch overwhelming all her senses. No other woman responds to my touch as quickly as Kai, and it's sexy as hell.

I want her to come over and over, until any thoughts of her painful first time are all but a distant memory.

She starts wiggling and panting so much I can tell she's close. Her thighs squeeze around my head; her grip on my head death-defying. I can barely breathe, let alone move, she has me so tightly in her grasp, but I've never been so happy to be suffocated by a woman before.

I dip my tongue into her tight cunt. Pushing deeper, preparing her for what will soon be coming—my cock.

I probably shouldn't fuck her again so soon after her first intrusion. I'm sure she's sore, but the way her wetness is already coating my tongue, I have no doubt she wants this.

"Make me come you fucking asshole!" she screams.

I pull my tongue out of her and move back to her clit.

She explodes.

"Enzo!" she cries over and over as she comes on my mouth, her orgasm rippling through her over and over. She throws her head back; it's like nothing exists. Zeke or Langston could walk in right now, and I don't think she'd notice or care.

"Baby, you are going to have to open your legs so I can move my head. My cock wants a turn."

She slowly relaxes, and I spread her legs apart wide enough to unlock my head from her grip.

"That didn't sound like someone who hated me."

Her eyes glisten. "I hate you."

"You may hate me, but you love my tongue. You love my body. But most of all, you love my cock."

I undo my pants, pull a condom from my pocket, and then drop my jeans, letting my cock free.

Her eyes immediately go to its large girth.

I smirk. I've been with women before who couldn't handle my size. They gave up and stopped, unable to handle the pain. Others suffer through but only after several painful moments stretching them out.

It still amazes me how Kai handles me. She's petite, and her pussy is no different than any other part of her.

"I don't love your cock," she whispers, but her eyes tell me differently. She loves it, but she's also scared based on how last time went.

I don't want her thinking about it. It won't help her to dwell on my past mistakes. She does better when she's just living in the moment.

"Tell me how much you fucking hate me, baby."

"I hate how fucking arrogant you are."

"Yea?" I trail kisses up her leg.

"I hate how incredibly bossy you are."

I kiss over her sensitive clit again, and she stops talking, focusing on the touch.

When I kiss her stomach, she starts again. "I hate how controlling you are."

My eyes grow large looking at her breasts again. I take my time tasting each luscious mound—kissing every part and ending, sucking on her hard nipples.

When I bite down, she squeals and tries to swat me

away. But I don't stop, loving the fucking sound of her squeals too much.

My cock grows another inch at the sound. I press at her entrance, my dick desperate to feel her tight lips welcoming me in. I consider fucking her bareback, but think better of it. She's not on birth control. And even if she were, I wouldn't risk it. I will never get a woman pregnant. *Ever.* This legacy dies with me.

I rip the condom wrapper open and lean back to slide it on, and then I'm pressing roughly at her entrance.

"And I hate how fucking big you are."

Our eyes gleam at each other, and then I grab her hips, jerk her from the counter, and flip her around so her ass is in the air and she's bent over the counter.

I slip halfway in while she's still adjusting to the new position, instead of giving her time to think about the pain. I kiss her neck and fist her hair giving her enough pain to focus on other than the ripping torment as I stretch her wide.

She winces and her pussy tightens, not used to my size yet.

It takes every drop of self-control inside me to not push in deeper like I need. But I won't hurt her like I did last time.

"How badly do you want to slap me right now?" I goad.

"So fucking badly."

She releases one of her arms from the counter, trying to reach back to do just that. I grab it and force it tightly behind her back.

"I love how feisty you are."

"I hate how cruel you are."

I lean down and kiss her palm as I move another inch

inside her. Her slickness swells from my kiss. "It seems you like how sweet I can be to you."

I suck each of her fingers, slipping another millimeter in with each distracting kiss.

"I fucking love your tits, baby."

I grab them roughly, my fingers teasing the points.

"Aw," she moans as I again descend into her tightness.

"How the fuck did you fit the last time?" she pants.

I ignore her question, knowing we need to focus on other things to get her to relax.

I kiss down her back, and I feel her body start to relax allowing more. So close.

"I can't. You're too fucking much," she groans.

"I didn't think you were a quitter, baby."

"I'm not."

"You got this. We are so close."

I'm failing. I don't want her feeling pain. I feel her body tensing and beginning to close up to me. If I were to look into her eyes, I'm sure they would be glossing over, preparing to protect herself as she has done for years before. Then she would never get to feel the pleasure.

Then I get an idea.

I slap her ass.

She yelps.

"And I fucking love this ass."

I rub gently over the redness from when I punished her last night.

"You didn't act like it last night," she pants.

I smile as she soaks my cock from thinking about last night.

I squeeze the reddened cheeks, and she cries out.

"You sadistic ass."

I hear the tiny tears.

Dammit.

"Look at me, baby."

She turns her head, and I see the tears. I kiss her cheeks, removing them from her eyes.

Then I suck two of my fingers. Her mouth parts as she stares at me. "But do you know what I love most of all?"

"My pussy."

"Yes. But I want something else more."

"What?"

"Your ass."

"What? No! I can't."

I press my fingers at the entrance to her ass, putting just enough of my fingers inside to get her to focus on a different sensation. I kiss her lips with everything I have, and then I grind into her body, sinking all of my cock inside.

The moan she cries into my mouth is beautiful. I love the pain, but most of all I love her pleasure.

Tears stain her cheeks, but I can already see the pain easing.

"I can do this. I want to. Jesus, Enzo. Fuck me."

I smile. "You've already taken me. All of me, baby."

Her eyes widen in surprise.

"Hang on," I say motioning to the counter.

She grabs on, and then I fuck her like I've wanted to since I came into the kitchen.

Her pussy welcomes me in more and more with each thrust, as I grip her ass and kiss every part of her bare neck.

"I love hearing you cry, baby."

"Because you are a sadist."

"No, because I love every fucking sound you make. Most of all when you scream my name."

I hit particularly deep inside, and I get exactly the reward I want. "Enzo!"

Her muscles start tightening, her body coming alive.

I reach around, find her clit, and start strumming her. I want her to come so many times that even if she had the highest powered vibrator, she would have nothing left to make herself come.

She arches her back, her ass pushing into my cock more. *Someday, I will have your ass.*

We build ourselves higher and higher in our little bubble. I cling on for dear life as I struggle to hold back my own orgasm until she comes. Fucking her, with how tight she is, brings me back to when I was fifteen and would shoot my load far too fast. Now, I never come before a woman. I may be heartless, but I'm not a bad lover.

I plead with my cock to hold on. *Wait until she comes.*

And then it happens. Her pussy contracts around me, her cries bounce through the house, and her body turns icy from the chill she sends through my body. The look on her face is glorious as she comes on my dick.

I pump one more time, and I lose it with her. I growl at the explosion I wish could last forever.

More, more, more.

The orgasm rolls through us both again. My heat shoots through her, and her ice through me. Only when I return to my usual warm, and she returns to her usual chill, do the orgasms stop.

"That was—Jesus, I never thought it could be like that," she says, repeating her same sentiment from before.

I pull out of her sharply, giving her no warning this time.

She doesn't wince this time though. She's too lost in her orgasm to feel the loss. I turn her to me and kiss her lips.

"No wonder you fuck so many women all the time if it's like that."

"It's not like that every time."

Her eyebrows raise, and she lights up.

Fuck, this woman. One sentence makes her happy.

"Now what?" she asks, innocently.

I stare down between her legs, happy to only see the tiniest drop of blood this time instead of the volcano of blood I caused last time.

She's getting used to my size, and I want to spend most of the night fucking her until we fall asleep completely exhausted. We should spend the night getting the best sleep, but there is no harm if we both get the same amount of sleep.

I'll make sure she gets at least six or seven hours, even though we both function pretty well without sleep.

"I could spend the night fucking you, if you aren't too sore?"

She gives me the slowest smile on the planet, but thank fuck I can read her well enough to answer.

"I'll happily hate-fuck you all night," she says.

19

KAI

WE FUCKED MOST of the night.

Maybe that was his plan to have an unfair advantage: fucking me so much I could barely walk. It worked. But I don't care, even if that was his plan. I wouldn't have traded the sex for anything.

I never knew how amazing sex could be—not until Enzo.

I thought it must be horrible—at least that's how my fucked up brain processed how the woman feels during sex. Because of Jarod and his goons. The screams the other women made will live in my head forever.

The torture of countless men pretending to go for my pussy then stop in disgust will live with me forever.

The pain at Enzo's size is a lot—but it's nothing compared to the moments after. The moments he tried to distract me from the pain. The moments he's sweet instead of the devil. The moments when it starts to feel good. *Really good.*

I'm sure sex with a different, smaller man would be less

painful, but I doubt any man has the talents of making me wet with solely a syllable like Enzo does.

We slept in the bed all night side by side, but not touching. As usual. I like Enzo's touch, but I'm still not completely calm every time he does it. It can still cause me panic or freak me out if I'm not ready for it. So at night, it's probably best if we don't snuggle.

And Enzo is used to sleeping alone. He has no need for a snuggle buddy.

We don't talk about it. It just happens. We just share his bedroom like an old married couple.

I stare down at Enzo's mother's ring on my hand as the alarm goes off. It's eight-thirty. Only a half hour until we have to be ready.

I don't want to be Enzo's friend today. It will make it harder to hurt him. And it will destroy me if he hurts me. Especially after our night of lovemaking.

He reaches across the bed and tucks my hair behind my ear.

I freeze.

That's too much—too caring. He shouldn't do things like that.

He's just trying to throw you off guard. Make you want him so you won't hurt him when it comes down to it.

Don't fall for his tricks.

I smile. "Morning."

"Morning," he sighs. "Sleep well?" the cocky grin on his face tells me he already knows I did.

I nod, continuing to play with the ring.

"When we get out of this bed, we are enemies again," he says.

"Agreed."

"Until then..." he reaches over and kisses me tenderly. I wonder how it would be to fuck him gently and tenderly. I always thought it would be too mushy and slow to keep my demons away. But after having him hard and rough, I want to find out what sex is like with Enzo in every way possible.

"Here," I say, taking the ring off and holding him out to him.

"Do you want a divorce already? I thought I was doing a good job satisfying you in my bed."

I smile. "No, I just don't want to have any loyalty to you once we get out of this bed. I'm not your fake wife today. I'm your enemy. And I don't want to accidentally lose it or something."

He takes the ring, but instead of putting it somewhere safe, he grabs my hand again and slips the ring back on.

"We can be enemies and fuck buddies. We can hate each other and still want each other. We can be adversaries and still care. I gave it to you to keep no matter what happens. It's yours—not mine. It's your leverage to protect you when the time comes for you to start your life over. I don't want you to forget I want you safe during the game. Because I do. I will do what I can to protect you."

"I don't want your protection."

"But you have it. I won't let anyone hurt you." He kisses the ring on my finger. "This is my promise. I will always keep you safe. No matter how we feel about each other. Our hate won't stop how I protect you."

I look at the clock. Five minutes have passed. We need to shower and eat something before the game starts.

"Good luck," I say.

"Good luck."

We both exit the bed at the same time. We don't talk. We

don't acknowledge the other as we get ready for the day. It's like a flip has been switched. Like we didn't just fuck each other's brains out all night. We have no connection anymore.

My stomach is in knots, so I don't eat much. I drink an iced coffee and pick at some eggs. I take as long as I can in the shower, letting the water wash away any remnants of Enzo. I can't think about him.

I get dressed in dark jeans, a tight fitting black shirt, and comfortable running shoes. I don't know what the task is, but I'd rather be ready for a fight than dressed for a ball.

I put my hair up in a high ponytail and decide on a no-makeup look.

I stare down at the ring, deciding to keep it on. Enzo's right, I might need to sell it for money at some point. And if today goes badly and I'm left abandoned in Mexico or something, then I might need to sell it sooner than later.

Then I head downstairs.

We are supposed to meet Archard at Surrender.

I assume Enzo will give me a ride since I don't have a car, money, or any other means of transportation.

"Miss Miller, Enzo is waiting for you in the car out front," Westcott says when I reach the main floor.

"Thanks."

"Good luck to you, Miss Miller," Westcott says as I approach the door.

I nod and step outside. His good luck didn't actually sound like a well-wishing of words. It sounded like a warning.

I step outside expecting to see one of Enzo's shiny race cars. Instead, I see a large blacked out SUV.

I approach the passenger side and see Zeke sitting there. Langston is in the driver's seat.

I smile at them and then walk to the second door and open it. Enzo is already seated on the far side. I climb in and shut the door.

None of the men speak to me, but Langston starts driving.

I can normally tolerate silence, but the silence is suffocating.

I stare at the men, all dressed similarly to my own look: dark jeans, dark T-shirts, and jackets. The only difference is I'm sure they are all caring guns, knives, and any other weapon they can hide beneath their clothing.

I try to forget about what's happening and stare out the window. I let the sun warm my face as I lean it closer to the glass.

Langston stops the car at the back entrance of Surrender. We all climb out one by one and file into the building, walking toward Enzo's office.

No, not his office. Black's office. This could as easily be my office as it is Enzo's.

I notice a large table has been brought in, and Archard is already sitting at one end.

Enzo walks around to one side of the table and takes a seat. Langston and Zeke follow. Zeke looks weak, his steps are careful, and I'm sure he's still feeling a lot of pain.

I take a seat opposite them and watch as the three men stare at me like I'm truly their enemy. I no longer feel welcome here. I knew Enzo would be staring at me with determination in his eyes, but Zeke and Langston's looks surprise me. I thought I had made headway in making them think better of me. But they are both glaring at me like they want to kill me and they are just waiting for their boss' word.

Archard nods to both of us and pulls out a piece of paper.

"I will read the rules, ask for any questions you may have, and then the game will start. Remember, outside of the rules I read; there are no rules. As long as you don't break the specific rules written here, you are free to win in any way possible."

Any way possible. His words read dark, and I know he means we can kill each other if that is how we'd like to win. I wouldn't be able to kill Enzo. For one, I don't even have a gun. I already know Enzo won't kill me. But could he order one of his men to do it?

"You are free to use any resources, people, etc. you can persuade to your side."

I stare across at Zeke and Langston. Enzo has the loyalty of two great men. They will do whatever they can to help him win. And he has a whole organization of people at his disposal that would help him.

As his fake wife, I might be able to convince a few of them to help me out. But I don't want help. I want to do this on my own.

I stare at the empty chairs next to me. *I'm alone. I'm always alone.*

"Now to the rules. The objective is easy: steal the high school class ring of Mr. Milo Wallace."

He opens the folder in front of him and pulls out two identical images and hands one to Enzo, the other to me.

I stare at the picture of a man's hand with a high school ring on his pinky.

What grown ass man still wears a high school ring?

"The ring has no value other than sentimentality to this man. The rules are simple. You can't take it by force or kill anyone in the process. You have to steal it in a way where he doesn't realize you were the one to steal it. If you get caught taking it, you lose automatically. The winner is the first person to steal it without being caught and without breaking the rules."

Steal, don't get caught, don't kill anyone.

I exhale a long breath. It's like this game was designed for me. I've spent my entire life stealing to survive. I'm a very good pickpocket. I've never been caught taking an item from someone. I've stolen watches, wallets, purses, jewelry; the list goes on. This will be the easiest task I've ever had.

I stare across at Enzo—my opponent. He's grown up in a life filled with criminals. But as far as I know, Enzo doesn't have any experience with thievery. He's never had to. He has limitless money, and men with fancy weapons to take whatever he wants.

I might actually have an advantage to this game. *Thank you, Dad.* He does love me. He did try to prepare me; he just never told me the truth.

I sigh in relief.

"One more thing," Archard says.

I freeze. I don't like the tone in which he said it.

"Enzo has already broken the rules by parading around as Black for years now, when it's clear he knew Kai was still alive."

Enzo's lips tighten.

"So you will have to face a penalty for that. I've thought long and hard about the appropriate penalty, and I've come up with a solution. Kai will have to agree to the terms, since your fathers never came up with a plan for such a situation.

"Enzo and any men he uses to complete this task will not be allowed to use weapons. No guns, no knives, nothing. You can carry nothing. You can not steal a weapon. If you get caught holding a weapon, you automatically lose this round." Archard looks to me for a response.

But I'm staring at Enzo. I've never known the man not to carry a gun. This would be a lot to ask of him, to not carry a weapon. For no other reason than he wouldn't want to put Zeke or Langston or any of his other men at risk.

But I won't be completing this task with a gun, so they might as well not either. It can't be that dangerous. We are just stealing a high school ring from some guy. It can't be that hard.

"I agree to the penalty," I say.

Enzo's vein in his head pops with frustration, but he just nods at Archard.

"Do you two have any questions about the rules or tasks?"

"Who is Milo Wallace?" I ask.

Archard shakes his head. "I'm sorry, but you will have to find out any information about this man yourselves. It's part of the task."

I stare across at Enzo who is tight-lipped. I'm sure he's heard of this man, if not Zeke or Langston will find out everything about him in a matter of minutes. That is where I will have a disadvantage. I have no access to men, computers, security. I don't have any money, nor a car, a cell phone, nothing.

Enzo will be able to get to Milo in a matter of minutes with ease. Giving him plenty of time to steal the ring before I even find out the man's address.

But once I find this man, I can steal it with ease.

"Any other questions?" Archard asks.

I shake my head. Enzo continues to sit silently.

"Good, then I'll be needing your weapons, Enzo," Archard says.

Enzo stares at me like he's going to kill me for this as he unloads his gun and knife. Langston does the same. Zeke hesitates for a minute. Maybe he's not carrying a gun because he's headed back to his bed after this.

"Zeke?" Archard asks.

Zeke pulls his gun from his pocket, but instead of laying it on the table, he gets up and walks to me.

He hands it to me. I take it hesitantly. He doesn't speak, but I can read his eyes easily. *Take it, stay safe; this is my forgiveness. This is all I'll do to help you.*

Then the men start filing out. Leaving me seated at the table by myself.

I stare at the ring one more time, memorizing it as I try to formulate a plan in my head. I've lived my life with nothing. No money, no car, nothing.

I stare down at the ring I could easily sell to give me all those things now in order to assist me this round and the rounds after.

No, I won't sell it. Only if my life depends on it. It means too much to Enzo. I could never hurt him like that. I still don't understand his compassion when he gave me the ring, but I know I have to keep the ring safe until he accepts it when I return it to him.

I can find a way to make this happen. I've spent my entire life with nothing and I more than survived.

There is a library a couple of blocks from here. I'll research everything I can on him and then form a plan. But I already know what that plan will have to involve. Milo Wallace is a man. I'm sure he's a powerful, rich man. There is only one way to ensure I can get close to him. Use my body to seduce him. It makes me sick to my stomach to think about flirting with a man after I just had a different man in my bed, but what choice do I have?

I don't know if I want to win. I don't know if I want to become Black. But if I lose, I'll end up with nothing. If I win, I'll have an entire empire at my disposal. If I win, I could change things. If I win, I could stop another woman from being sold. If I win, I could end the pain.

20

ENZO

KAI COULD WIN THIS.

And it scares the crap out of me. I've worked too hard, for too long to give her a chance at winning a single round. Everything would be destroyed if she won. I can't let it happen.

I sit in the passenger seat, while Zeke rides in the back, already on his computer looking things up about Milo Wallace. Langston is usually better at surveillance, but Zeke is too hurt to drive. And I need to be free to focus on formulating a game plan.

Zeke starts rambling everything we know about Milo, "He's wealthy—a one billion dollar fortune. He got all his money selling weapons. He's single, a perpetual bachelor. He lives in France but loves to sail his yacht. He's actually in Miami; he's throwing a big party tomorrow night on his yacht."

I take in all the information Zeke just gave me. In some ways, it would have been better if Milo was in France. Kai has no money to buy a plane ticket, and by the time she came up with the money to buy a ticket, I would have already flown my private jet to steal the stupid ring and be back.

But he's not in France, he's here, on his yacht. That's the second best news. Kai is afraid of yachts and the water. She won't go near him. That gives me an advantage. I'm not sure if he's the kind of man to step foot in Miami, or if he prefers the luxury of his yacht. I can't imagine a man like him ever leaving his yacht. So if she wants to win, she will have to face her fears.

I smirk. I know she's capable, but she might stall. Waiting him out to see if he will come to land first. That will give me a day's advantage.

"Where is he now?" I ask Zeke.

"He's anchored a few miles off the coast. They won't dock until tomorrow evening just before the party. He's a paranoid guy and feels safer on his yacht than on land."

I smile. *Perfect*.

I can easily get an invitation to this party. If I weren't already so focused on this game and Kai, I would have probably already ensured I had an invitation. This is the kind of man I want control and power over. I would have learned everything, found his weakness and exploited it until I was sure I could control him. That's what I do.

My mind spins with ideas of what I should do. But I know there is only one fool-proof way to get Milo alone—a woman.

If I was allowed a gun, I could easily persuade him to talk to me, but I'm not allowed one. Something I'm very pissed about. Kai should have never allowed that stupid penalty. I don't care about my life, but I will not put my men in danger.

"What's the plan, boss?" Langston asks. I share every-thing with him, and he's usually more involved in the planning and plotting process, instead of being stuck behind the wheel.

"Get an invite to the party tomorrow night," I answer.

"Already done," Zeke says.

I grin. Maybe Zeke is as good at plotting as Langston and I are. I just always think of Zeke as brute force, instead of brains.

"Then make sure I have the hottest date on my arm so Milo will want to talk with me. If for no other reason than to steal my date."

"Good plan, but then what? Do you know how to steal a ring without him noticing you are taking it?"

I shake my head. I don't have a clue. I've never stolen a wallet, let alone a ring. A ring seems impossible to steal.

"Kai might try to steal it from his finger in broad daylight, but that's not my plan. I could never take the ring from his finger without him noticing. No, my choices are to get him to bet it during a poker game. Or have my date take it during sex."

Langston raises an eyebrow. "Do you have a girl in mind that would be up for the task?"

"Yes," I sigh. I just hate asking her, because I know she'll say yes. She would do anything for me. And she's hot enough that Milo will be dying to get his hands on her.

Get him drunk.

Try to get him to play a poker game.

If that doesn't work, send in my date to seduce him.

Fuck, I hate the plan. But right now, it's all I've got.

"The invitation allows for a plus one. I know Milo won't allow you a security detail. But Langston and I will watch guard from the shore," Zeke says.

I don't know how to say this, but I have to. "You aren't coming, Zeke."

"What? You are not going by yourself."

"I won't. Langston will come and watch from as close as he can get, but I'm not putting you at risk."

"I can handle myself."

"You can when you are healthy. But you aren't allowed a weapon, and I don't want to be worried the entire time someone will shoot you again. You stay; I'm not going to discuss it anymore."

Zeke huffs but doesn't argue anymore. Langston gives me a look of thanks.

I turn to Langston. "You will carry a concealed weapon."

"What?"

"No one will know what you choose or where you hide it except you."

"But that's breaking the rules."

"Your life is more important than the rules. I won't carry anything, but I want you safe. Under no circumstances will you use it to save my life. Only yourself. Understand? Otherwise, you can stay back with Zeke."

"Understood, boss," Langston says, only calling me boss when he knows I'm serious.

I pull out my phone knowing I need to get my date figured out as soon as possible. I need to prepare her for the task so we practically share the same brain because I won't be able to change the plan very easily otherwise.

I scroll through the contacts until I find the one. I haven't called her in a few months. I've been too busy dealing with Kai, but there was a time when this girl was my everything. And that's exactly how she's listed in my phone.

My everything.

I hit the contact and wait.

Liesel's voice shines through the phone making it

impossible not to smile at her light voice even though I know I'm risking her life by doing this.

"What does my favorite guy want?" she asks immediately, but her voice isn't mad. She's happy I called.

"Why do you assume I want something?"

"Because I know you. You are all business. If I want to see you outside of work, I call you. So what do you need?"

God, this is why I can always count on Liesel.

"I need you to be my date," I say the words I know will make Liesel's year. Because even if the date is fake, it won't feel like that to either of us.

21

KAI

I'VE SPENT an hour in the library learning everything I can about Milo Wallace.

He's rich.

He's single, but always has a hot woman on his arm.

He lives in France.

But he's going to be here in Miami, tomorrow night.

And of course, he's throwing a party on his fancy yacht.

Shit.

Why does it have to be on a yacht?

This will be my only chance to get the ring. Flying to France would be an automatic loss. Enzo will have a private jet fly him before I can even figure out how to buy a ticket myself.

I need an invite to that party. I need a dress. I need the best hair and makeup. And then I need to seduce this man.

I could go to my father for help. But even if he wanted to help me, he has no money. And I don't want his help. He had twenty years to try and help me; he chose not to. He chose to keep me in the dark.

I could go back to Enzo's place, but I hate that idea. I'm

sure there is a fancy dress in the closet I could wear, but I don't want his help either.

I want to do this myself.

My wheels turn in my head trying to figure out a plan. *Think, think, think.*

I hate stealing things, but I don't have much of a choice.

I could use the gun tucked into my pants that Zeke gave me to rob someone, but that seems too dangerous. I should just stash the gun somewhere, because I know I'm not going to use it.

I stare down at the ring.

Sell it, pawn it.

No.

I turn the ring, trying to come up with a plan that doesn't make me a thief.

Ring!

I have my mother's ring in my jewelry box at my father's home. He gave it to me when she died. It won't get me as much money as Enzo's ring, but it will be enough to buy a slutty dress, some makeup, and a cab ride to the pier.

Two hours later, I have my mother's ring in my hand. A ring I never thought I would sell, even for food. But here I am standing outside the old pawn shop I've sold things at before, considering doing just that.

Sell Enzo's instead, the devil says in my ear.

No.

I don't need my mother's ring to remember her. And I will not betray Enzo by pawning his mother's ring off the first chance I get.

I take Enzo's ring off and slip it into my pocket. I don't want Jim to see it and try to convince me to pawn it to him.

The door chimes as I step inside, warning my heart of what I'm going to give up for a chance at winning. I'm selling a part of my heart I will never be able to get back. Then I'm going to dress like a slut so I can get let into a party I'm not invited to. All for a chance to seduce a man, so I can get close enough to steal a different ring. Maybe I'll be able to pawn Milo's ring in order to get this one back, but I doubt it.

I have to think of the real reason I'm sacrificing my heart in order to win: to keep other women from getting hurt. Because once I'm Black, I can change everything.

22

ENZO

Damn.

That's all that goes through my mind when I pick up Liesel in my Ferrari.

She descends from the doorway of the condo building she lives in in a black dress with a low V-neck down the front and shiny, sparkly shoes. Her hair is down in long curls, and she's wearing the expensive necklace I bought her years ago when we were dating.

"You look good," I say as I lean against my car.

She eyes my tux, practically undressing me with her smoldering eyes. "I know."

I grin.

Liesel always is one of the most confident women I know. She knows what she wants and she goes after it. And she won't settle for less than. Which is why we aren't together. I know she wants me, but I couldn't give her what she needed or deserved, so we broke up.

Looking at Liesel now, most men would say I made an error not giving her everything she wanted, marriage included, but looking at how Liesel is dressed just confirms to me I made the right decision. *She's dangerous.*

Dangerous in a different way from Kai. Kai unnerves me; she makes me think twice about my decisions and actions; she makes me want things I never knew I wanted. Makes me want to protect her even when she doesn't need my protection.

But Liesel is just pure sex. She doesn't want me to change. She would take me exactly as I am, dangerous job and all. She likes rough sex. She likes my fancy cars. My big beach house. She likes going to expensive parties. She's likes being rich and flaunting everything she has.

Kai couldn't care less about my money. She would trade her living situation for a second to get free. The only money she needs is enough to survive.

"Ready?" I ask.

Her eyes sear into me and her red lips plump. "You know it."

I walk around to the driver's side, not bothering to open Liesel's door. I'm not an asshole to Liesel, but I don't want her getting the wrong idea. She already will when I have to fake being into her.

The truth is, I look at Liesel as more as a sister than a potential wife. Yes, we used to date. Yes, I find her attractive. But she is also the only woman I could ever confide in. The only woman I could ever have real conversations with. And I wouldn't trade that for anything. I will protect her and care for her all of my life.

We both climb in, and I start driving, with Langston trailing behind for protection.

"So I'm here. Dressed to the nines as requested."

"You always dress to the nines, Liesel."

She smiles. "I do, but why did you need me to?"

I sigh. I told her just enough to get her to go with me, nothing more. "Because you are my date."

"Who am I trying to make jealous?"

"No one."

"Then, why am I coming?"

"I need a hot woman on my arm to get a man to want you."

"So I'm a distraction?"

"A hot distraction, yes."

"And, why am I a hot distraction?"

"Because I need to steal a ring."

She raises an eyebrow. "You could just buy a ring."

I stare at her silently, and as usual, she can read my thoughts. "You found her."

"Yes. Well technically, she found me. Kai came back."

She nods. "What do you need me to do?"

"I already told you."

She shakes her head. "I don't want you to lose everything you've worked so hard to gain. Everything your entire life has been about. You were basically born Black. You have never been Rinaldi; I will do anything to help you retain the title. So tell me the truth. What do you need me to do?"

I sigh. There is no bullshitting Liesel; she knows me too well. "I will do everything possible to get the ring. Bet him in a poker game. *Anything*. But if I can't..." I can't say the words.

She smirks. "Say it Black."

"I can't."

She shakes her head. "You always were a pussy. You want me to get him in bed and steal the ring."

I nod.

She smiles. "Who is this man?"

I pull out my phone and pull up the image of him.

"Jesus! He's fucking hot and rich!"

I nod.

"Done," she says. "I'd fuck him for free."

I exhale a deep breath. *Thank God.* If it came down to it, I wouldn't be able to force her to fuck someone she didn't want to. But Liesel likes men and sex. I figured this would be an easy sell. And even though I know she would do anything for me, she wouldn't spread her legs only to help me.

She continues studying the phone on the ride to the pier. Learning everything she can about Milo Wallace.

"We're here. I don't think it will come down to it." I take her hand and squeeze.

"Stop thinking about me as a girl. I like sex. And this man is hot. It wouldn't really be a hardship if I had to. I might do it regardless of if you need me to or not." She winks as the valet opens her door.

I step out and walk to her after talking with the valet. My eyes trail around in the dark looking for Langston, but I can't spot him, which means he's hidden well.

I hold out my arm, and she takes it. She leans in and smiles, making it easily look like we are a real couple. We have that kind of connection.

We board the yacht, and everyone's eyes turn to us. Between my powerful stance and Liesel's sexy dress, we demand attention.

"We still got it," I say leaning into Liesel's ear.

She beams and squeezes my arm. "We do make a good couple."

"Would you like a drink?"

"Do you even have to ask?"

I lead Liesel over to the bar. I get her champagne, not

Betrayed by Truths

because it's her favorite, but because it looks sexy as hell when she drinks it. And I get a scotch.

"So, this bitch, do you think she will show up tonight?" Liesel asks.

"She has a name and you know it."

She shrugs. "I do, but I prefer to think of her as a bitch."

"She's not a bitch. She is as trapped in this situation as I am."

She stops her drink inches from her lips and studies me. "Do you have a thing for this girl?"

"No, I just don't want anything to happen to her. I protect her like I protect anyone else who is innocent."

"You like her." She shakes her head.

"No, I don't. She's my prisoner."

She raises an eyebrow. "When did that happen?"

"When she lost a bet to me and ended up in my house. I will only let her go free when we finish this stupid game. That way I can control her and keep an eye on her."

"So where is she now?"

I shrug. "Probably trying to figure out how to get her nerve up to get an invite to this party."

She cocks her head, not understanding.

"She's afraid of yachts."

"Interesting."

I shrug, and then I spot Milo.

He has a woman on each arm, a cigar hanging from his lips, and a scotch in hand.

"Game time," I say, nodding in his direction with my eyes.

Liesel's eyes cut over.

"Damn, he's hotter in person."

"And he already has two women you'll have to compete with."

237

She pushes her boobs up and flips her hair. "Those bitches aren't any competition."

Liesel leans into me, nuzzling my neck, before she lets her tongue circle the rim of my ear.

My body heats, but nothing more. My cock doesn't even flinch. I'm on a mission, and nothing this woman does will affect me.

But it does Milo.

As if he has an alarm out that goes off whenever a hot woman does anything around him, he locks eyes on us.

Well, Liesel to be exact.

I thumb her bare neck, showing him what he could have but doesn't.

Milo shakes off both women, excusing them with just a word.

"Damn, you're good."

Her eyes don't leave mine. "I know."

Milo walks over to us. "Mr. Black, I'm so happy you could attend." He holds his hand, and I shake it, immediately noticing his high school class ring on his pinky as I expected.

I nod, "This yacht is something else."

He smirks. "It would be since you built it."

"I did."

Milo turns his attention to Liesel who is still clinging to me like she wants to fuck me in the bathroom.

"And who is your date, Black?" Milo asks.

I wait; Liesel isn't the type of woman who waits for a man to introduce her.

"I'm Liesel Dunn; it's a pleasure to meet you, Milo Wallace," she says before licking her bottom lip. Her breasts seem to have gotten bigger in the moment since Milo walked over as she presses them up in her dress.

They shake hands, but Milo's hand lingers in Liesel's. His eyes drop to her chest, looking in an obvious way.

"My eyes are up here, Milo," Liesel says, catching him staring.

Milo doesn't apologize, he just peers into her eyes, as lost in them as he was in her breasts. *This will be too easy.*

"The yacht leaves in twenty minutes, as soon as all the guests arrive. There will be drinking, dancing, fireworks. The whole bit. Save me a dance, Liesel."

"I'm not sure I can be torn away from Black here," she twirls her hand into the base of my hair.

But Milo is no longer watching her displays of affection; he's looking at Liesel like she's a piece of meat he wants to devour. Being on my arm makes no difference to him. A man like him is used to getting what he wants. He's rich and good looking enough to usually get his way.

But then he's looking past her and his eyes heat even more.

I turn in the direction of his gaze.

Holy fuck.

Kai.

She's on the yacht.

How the fuck?

I notice her body first. *How could I not?*

She's in a blue-green dress. The same color as the sea and her eyes. Every other woman here is wearing black, silver, or red—not Kai. The color she chose stands out above the rest.

It should make her look childish because the color isn't usually associated with being womanly. But it doesn't.

It makes her look like the ocean itself. It fits her snugly, like it was made to drape over her skin. Accenting her flat stomach, perky breasts, and curvy ass.

A slit rides high up her thigh, and although the dress shows her cleavage, she's not showing as much as Liesel. But it doesn't fucking matter.

Because she looks so goddamn beautiful.

She swept her hair up and wears an innocent amount of makeup in contrast to every other woman here.

It's like she took the perfect woman and did the opposite but somehow came out looking even hotter because she's so different.

I finally catch the look on her face, and it ends me.

She's biting her damn lip and tucks a loose curl behind her ear. Her eyes cut side to side as if danger is all around her. I can feel her heart racing from here.

Her eyes are bulging, allowing the blue from them to pop even more.

She's terrified to be on this yacht, but she's doing it anyway. And that makes her even sexier.

Every man is staring at her, much in the same way they did Liesel when we first arrived. But this is different. She came alone, so the sharks will start circling faster. And her big doe-eyes showing her innocence make men respond in a way they never will to a woman like Liesel.

Men know Liesel is experienced. She'll be fire in bed.

Men know Kai has never been touched. And they want to teach her everything.

They don't know I've already had her. She's as strong as ice but way more inviting. She'd be the best they ever had.

Kai finally spots me. And her timid gaze turns to frigid in a second when she sees Liesel all over me.

I wince. She'll make me pay for that later, I'm sure. Or worse, she will never let me touch her again for bringing a beautiful woman here to do exactly what she's planning on doing—seducing Milo.

She doesn't hold my gaze long. Because she's locked in on her target—Milo.

And he's already smitten.

Fuck.

My only hope now is that Milo thinks stealing a woman from a powerful man like me is more entertaining than the angel that looks like she was born from the sea. Because if not, I'm fucked. If Kai gets so much as a moment alone with him, she will steal his ring with ease. And I'll be down one to nothing.

23

KAI

I see red when I see Enzo with that woman.

Of course, he would bring the hottest fucking woman to this party. And of course, she would be all over him. I would be all over him if I could.

She's not his prisoner.

She has nothing to lose by being with him.

While every time I let him fuck me, I lose more of myself—especially my pride.

I was terrified when I had the Uber drop me off in front of the yacht. For one, I didn't think I would be let aboard. But the security guard didn't even ask for my name to check against his list. He took one look at me and practically escorted me personally aboard. He let me know Mr. Wallace would love to see me in the VIP room as soon as we set sail.

And then I stepped onto the yacht, and everything came back.

The rocking of the boat.

The beatings, whippings, blood.

The pain, agony, and fear.

The women's screaming.

All of it.

I might have pushed it away when Enzo fucked me, but it all came pouring back in at the first opportunity.

But when I spotted Enzo, it all disappeared again, at least for a moment. Because all I felt was fire.

I force my eyes away, needing a moment without the pain of seeing him with another woman.

Enzo isn't mine. I shouldn't care, but I do.

The man my eyes land on are those of my target—Milo Wallace.

My lips part looking at the man who drips sex, much in the same way Enzo does.

This man is older though, by at least five years. But he carries himself with Enzo's same cocky attitude.

And his desire shines when he looks at me.

He wants me.

That was easy.

I let my eyes drop in a bashful way, knowing I look out of place and my only hope of drawing him over is to play innocent.

It works.

I see the shine of his shoes stop in front of me.

"I'm Milo Wallace. And you are fucking gorgeous."

My eyes slowly drift up to meet his.

I blush.

"I'm Kai Miller."

He holds out his hand as I knew he would. I don't let myself hesitate. I put my hand in his, swallowing down the pain at his touch.

I thought maybe a handsome man like Milo might be able to get through my defenses like Enzo does, but it's not Enzo's hotness that gets through. It's his caring, charming way he protects me even when he wants to hurt me.

"It's a pleasure to meet you, Miss Miller," he says holding my hand tightly as he leans down and kisses the top of it. "You are by far the most beautiful woman on my ship."

"Just your yacht? I figured you would call me the most beautiful woman in the world if you are going to feed me a line so cheesy," I say, trying to keep my confidence up as my hand burns with his touch.

I force the smile to stay on my lips and the twinkle in my eyes to remain, despite wanting to get off this boat as quickly as possible.

My words only intensify his desire. I can see it in his eyes, and the bulge in his pants.

Jesus, what am I getting myself into? This man is going to want to fuck me and who knows how many other women. I won't be able to spread my legs if it comes down to it. And as soon as we leave the dock, I'm screwed. I won't have a choice to leave if he wants me. That's why men like him prefer the water to land. On the water, everyone is forced to play by his rules.

"I will have to work on my charm if I'm to be worthy of a woman like you."

I let my eyes smoke trying to show desire instead of fear.

"Excuse me, Mr. Wallace. We need you to approve we are ready to set sail and confirm all guests are on board," a man in a uniform says to Milo.

"Of course," Milo looks at me. "But I can already tell you the only guest that matters has just arrived." He winks at me.

He slowly releases my hand, and I can breathe again.

"I have business to attend to, unfortunately. I'll only be

gone a few minutes." He turns to his staff member. "Ensure Miss Miller has a drink and whatever else she wants and that she finds her way to the VIP room."

"Yes, Mr. Wallace."

Milo walks away, and the staff member remains staring at me. "What can I get you to drink, Miss Miller?"

I consider for a second. The woman on Enzo's arm is drinking champagne and looks sexy as hell. If I were smart, I'd drink the same. It's a light drink I will be able to tolerate without getting too drunk. It's a girly drink I would be expected to drink. But it's not what I want. I used to be able to keep up drinking with the best of men. Six years going without a drink have made me unable to tolerate liquor, but tonight I'm afraid I'm going to need the strength of alcohol to get me through this.

"Scotch. Get me your best scotch."

The staff member disappears to get what I demanded.

"I wasn't sure you were going to make it," Enzo says startling me.

How he can sneak up on me so easily drives me mad.

I turn to him with a large smile on my face.

"Doubting my abilities already? Not smart on your part," I answer.

Enzo doesn't hide his desire from me when he stares at me with large eyes even though his date is still hanging all over him.

"I would never doubt you."

"Good."

We both stare. Neither of us backing down.

"Introduce me, Enzo."

Enzo frowns at his date's comment, but I don't know why. I want to be introduced to the bitch.

"Liesel, this is Kai," Enzo says.

I smile when he introduces me as Kai instead of Katherine.

I hold out my hand, wanting to grip this woman's hand.

She takes it, and then her eyes grow big when she spots the ring. I moved the ring from my left hand to the right so Milo wouldn't know I am fake married. And I'm going by Kai Miller instead of Katherine Black, so hopefully, the news of our fake marriage hasn't spread to Milo yet. I don't know how much he knows Enzo. But as far as I know, Enzo hasn't spread news of our marriage to anyone. And I've only told a handful of people at Surrender.

She throws my hand down and stares at Enzo. "You didn't."

Enzo takes a second to see what Liesel was staring at. "We aren't legally married or married in any real way. I thought a fake marriage might be necessary for the men to accept her authority at Surrender, but I'm not sure it's the best idea anymore. We had pictures taken and everything to announce our rushed wedding, but I haven't released them yet. The only person who knows about our fake marriage is dead. So we have time to decide how to handle it."

Liesel shakes her head, not caring about any of his words. "I fucking know you aren't married you asshole. That's not what I'm mad about."

"Then what?"

"You gave her your mother's ring."

My eyes widen. *How does she know that?* This woman isn't just a fling he brought here to make Milo jealous. This woman knows a lot. She didn't seem surprised to see me or ask too many questions. She now knows about our fake marriage Enzo might not even be sharing with the world. And she knows about his mother's ring.

"I did. She needed a security policy in case something happens."

Liesel drops her fascade and crosses her arms glaring at him. "She doesn't deserve your protection. And she sure as hell doesn't deserve your ring."

"Excuse me, sorry to interrupt," the staff member from before says.

He holds out my scotch. "Here is your drink, Miss Miller."

"Thank you," I say taking it and realizing I need it more than I realized.

"Mr. Wallace has requested all of your presence in his VIP room. When you are ready, I can escort you."

I take a deep breath as the yacht starts moving. It's so slow it shouldn't affect me, but it does. My stomach immediately churns, threatening to throw up. I try downing the scotch in my hand, but once the liquid is in my belly I realize it won't help. My stomach keeps churning with the gentle rocking of the ship.

"If you could show me to the restroom first, I would appreciate it; then I'll be ready to go to the VIP room," I answer.

"Of course, right this way Miss Miller."

I hand him my empty glass and follow, forgetting all about Liesel and Enzo.

He leads me to a private section of the boat, then opens the door to the restroom.

"I'll get you another drink," he says with a small smile. "You can head through that door if I haven't returned by the time you are finished." He nods in the direction of a door at the end of the hallway.

I wince, trying to keep myself together.

"Thank you," I mumble and duck inside. I slam the door shut and lean against it just before I fall apart.

The panic attack has me in full swing. My body trembles against the door, my stomach heaves, and I know I'm seconds away from throwing up everything inside, my body twisting in torture.

I feel the ice cold shiver in my spine pulling me to shut down. Shut it all down. It's the only way to save myself.

A tear falls down my cheek. I'm stronger than this. I have to be. If I shut down, there is no guarantee I will be able to leave this bathroom. I'll fail without even really trying.

I can't.

My breathing is fast and uncontrollable, but even so, I can't get enough air in my lungs. My head is pounding. And then my stomach wretches.

I run to the toilet and vomit.

Everything comes up until my stomach has emptied.

I hear a knock on the door.

Shit. The staff member. *Why didn't I get his name?*

"I'm fine," I shout, hoping that's enough to get him to leave.

And then I vomit again. I grip the toilet, hating that even though I'm wearing one of the most beautiful dresses, I'm sick.

Please don't let me get anything on the dress.

The door opens, and my panic rises to a new level.

No one can see me like this.

And then I see the dark eyes of a man who's seen me come numerous times now. A man I'm far too intimate with. A man I'm pissed at.

"Just leave. You win. I won't be able to leave this bathroom until we stop moving," I say.

Enzo shuts the door behind him.

"I'm not winning like this."

I sigh. But then I can't think because I'm dry heaving over the toilet.

When my stomach seems to stop, Enzo holds out his hand, and I take it until I'm standing up.

"Here," he says holding out his own scotch to me.

I take it and swig a few sips back to wash my mouth of the taste of vomit. Then I move to the sink to wash my face.

My stomach is empty, but I still feel like a wreck.

"Go," I try again. "Steal the ring. You win."

"No, that's not why I'm here. I'm not here to gloat."

"Then, why are you here?"

His eyes heat. "To fuck you in that dress."

Everything stops when he says that. And then I finally come to my senses and laugh. "I think your date might get a little jealous."

He shakes his head. "I don't want my date; I want you."

I chuckle quietly. "I just vomited, my face is flushed, I'm ice cold and shivering. In a few minutes, I won't even realize what is happening anymore because I'll have shut everything out. You don't want me."

Enzo grabs my hips and forces me in front of him at the mirror.

"Look at yourself. I don't see a woman who just vomited out of weakness. I see fierce eyes, determined not to shut down. I see warm cheeks and a strong exterior. I seek a kick-ass woman who faced her fears, walked onto this yacht, and captured the attention of every man on the boat, including Milo. And more importantly, me."

I shake my head. "Stop trying to make me feel better."

He presses my ass to his front, and I feel how hard his cock is.

"Does this feel like a man who isn't turned on by you?"

He's hard as steel.

"I'm sure Liesel helped you along."

He growls and pulls me harder against him. "You have no idea how beautiful you are. You are fucking incredible. Liesel was all over me, and I didn't want her. You stood and batted your eyes across the room, and I've been hard and aching ever since."

I breathe out shallow breaths. Wetness pours into my panties. And my heart stops.

"Now, help a man out and fuck me."

I gasp.

"Fuck me, Kai. I need to fuck you. I can't go all night watching you with Milo and not having you first. I want my cum dripping from your pussy every time you smile at him. I want you sore from my cock every time you move a muscle to flirt with him. I want you thinking of me every time you talk to him. Now, fuck me."

I swallow hard. I can't believe he said that to me.

"Fuck me, Enzo."

He growls again. "My pleasure."

His lips go to my bare neck immediately, and every other feeling melts away as his lips ravish me.

I forget about my mission.

I forget about my anxiety.

I forget about Liesel.

It's just me and Enzo.

"God, the second you walked on this yacht I got jealous as hell. I didn't want any man looking at you, let alone touching you."

"No one touched me."

His eyes rage. "Milo touched you."

I smile. "He only touched my hand."

He grabs my hand and brings it to his lips. "This is my hand."

"Oh really?" I smirk.

He runs his hands over the front of my dress, stopping on my breasts. "These are mine."

He kisses my shoulder. "This skin is mine."

His hand trails down the side to my waist and ass. He begins pulling up my dress until he can feel my ass. "This ass is mine."

I hear a zipper and assume he's pulling his large cock out. I'm not scared about it fitting. Not this time. I'm soaked thinking about him. And I'm as desperate for him as he is for me.

He pushes my panties aside, and then I feel him pushing at my entrance.

"Mine," he says as he plunges into me.

I cry out, but not in pain. There is some agony, but mostly it's a territorial and primal need to claim him as much as he's claiming me.

"Fuck," I moan as he sinks in deeper, while his hand reaches around to find my clit.

I feel myself climbing high, and we've only barely gotten started.

I'm panting, wet, and needy and his cock is barely inside me.

"More."

"Baby, you're not ready."

"More, Enzo." I meet his eyes in the mirror, and I know he's losing control. He can't hold back any longer.

I bite my lip, daring him with his eyes. He finally gives me what I want. *All of him.*

"Mine," I cry out, taking all of him.

Our eyes meet again. "You're all mine," I say, again,

making it clear if I'm his, then he's mine. He doesn't get to go to that slut tonight after our mission is over.

"I'm fucking yours," he says.

I smile.

And then he fucks me like he's lost all control.

Driving in and out of me with a frenzy I haven't seen before.

I grip the counter and match him thrust for thrust.

It's so much and not enough at the same time.

"Hang on, baby," he says understanding immediately what I need.

He picks up speed, thrusting harder, faster switching the angle until he's hitting that delicious spot inside me.

"Enzo," I cry. *How can it get better each time he fucks me?* I didn't think it could keep feeling better, but it does.

"I could listen to you say my name all fucking night."

"Yes, Enzo," I cry again, barely registering his words or anything else.

"Are you about to come, baby?"

"Yes," I whisper, no longer able to speak, breathe, or move. All I can do is feel intensity as he fucks me into oblivion.

"Then come, baby."

"I'm coming," I cry a second later, loving that his words sent me into my orgasm.

His meets me at the same time, and I feel his orgasm shooting inside me.

Slowly we still, coming down from our high. Enzo pulls out of me, and I straighten my dress out.

"Mine," he says again, winking at me. And then he exits the bathroom. Leaving me to compose myself before I leave.

I stare at myself in the mirror and smile. Realizing I don't feel sick any more thanks to Enzo. I don't know if that was his intention or if he just really needed to fuck me. But either way, I'm grateful.

And then I feel it—his cum staining my panties.

Shit.

He fucked me without a condom.

You can't get pregnant after one time, can you? You can if you fuck a man like Enzo.

I take a deep breath. I can't get pregnant, not on top of everything else. The sex is great, but I'm still his captive. He's still a monster. And we are still competing for everything.

He would make the worst father.

And I don't ever want to be a mother.

I'll take the morning after pill tomorrow. Right now, I have a ring to steal.

24

ENZO

FUCKING KAI WAS A MISTAKE.

Because when she came to the VIP room, she glowed and hasn't stopped since.

Milo hasn't arrived yet, but his dozen closest guests fill the rear rooms and upper deck, a deck with the best view on the yacht.

And Kai has been munching on a meat and cheese plate in the corner, while drinking her scotch and ignoring me.

Liesel, on the other hand, hasn't stopped asking me questions. "What did Kai say when you went after her?"

"Can I get you another drink?" I ask, ignoring Liesel.

She sighs. "If I'm going to have to keep dealing with you ignoring me, then yes."

Wanting to get Liesel a drink has nothing to do with Liesel and everything with wanting to be near Kai, who is standing at the bar munching on small bites of food to settle her stomach.

She was an absolute wreck when I entered the bathroom. Being on that yacht for all those years truly fucked her up. And it makes me pissed off for my part in it all.

Kai spots me walking toward her and smiles before she realizes what she's doing. She immediately stops. And starts walking away.

Dammit.

I retrieve drinks for Liesel and myself, only just returning to her side when Milo enters.

The room stops, staring at him.

"Thank you all for joining me. We are going to have one incredible night. Enjoy yourselves."

Everyone applauds him, like he's a fucking rock star or something.

Liesel resumes her flirting with me, by wrapping my arm around her waist and leaning into my chest.

Milo notices and starts approaching us, until Kai laughs loudly at something a gentleman next to her said. She hadn't been talking to the man until Milo entered. But I recognize him. He's Abel Frost. Wealthy, powerful, and handsome. Only third behind myself and Milo in wealth and good-looks.

I shake my head. Of course, she found the best looking man here to make Milo and me jealous.

I move to take a step toward her, but Liesel grabs my tie, stopping me. I'm not sure if it was intentional or if she is just continuing her flirting.

Milo abruptly turns in her direction instead of ours when he hears her infectious laugh. Every man in the room turns toward her like she's a siren calling their names.

"Shit, we have to do something," I say to Liesel.

"Just give him a moment to talk to her. He'll get bored soon enough, and then we will have our chance."

I shake my head. "You don't understand. She's a thief."

"Well, I could have guessed that. She's horrible."

"No, I mean she's stolen dozen of times to survive

growing up. When we first met, she stole my watch without me noticing. She has a gift for pickpocketing. If she gets even a second with him privately, she'll steal the ring before I have a chance at taking it."

"Shit," Liesel says back.

"That's not helpful. We need to do something, now."

I try to think, but I can't. Not as he nears my woman.

"I have an idea," Liesel says as Kai smiles at Milo.

Fuck.

"Fine, whatever. Just do it now."

"I'll be happy to."

She grabs my face and pulls me into a kiss. I haven't kissed this woman in over a year, but she kisses me like we were making out yesterday. I close my eyes, trying to make the kiss feel real, but all I can focus on is Kai.

And how wrong this feels.

We start moving, stumbling through the crowd. *How the hell will this help?*

And then we crash into someone.

"Oh my gosh! I'm so sorry. Sometimes I just let the passion get the best of me," Liesel says.

That's when I realize who we stumbled into—Milo and Kai.

Kai no longer looks charming. The anger is clear on her face, and there is no hiding it. She's pissed at Liesel for kissing me.

While Liesel on the other hand, looks smug and happy.

"I completely understand," Milo says swimmingly to Liesel, and my anger at Liesel's stunt dissipates.

I pull Liesel to me harder, knowing it will throw Kai off her game while also making Milo crave Liesel more.

"When you find the person you desire, everything else just disappears," Milo says, but his gaze soon turns from

Liesel to Kai, indicating Kai is the woman he's chosen for tonight.

Fuck, fuck, fuck.

I need to get him away from Kai now, before he falls any further for her.

"How about a game of poker? I haven't played in years, and I've heard you are the best."

"Nah, I'm good. You are welcome to play. There is a table set up downstairs," Milo says.

In the main rooms, not the VIP area.

Milo continues to stare at Kai like she's the only one in the room.

"I have a cuban, I'd love to smoke. Would you care to join me?" I ask.

Milo looks at me for a second. "After the fireworks, I always enjoy a good cuban after hearing that racket."

The fireworks aren't happening until much later in the night. I've played all of my cards. I don't know what else I can do short of throwing Liesel in between them.

"Will you show me the top deck? I would love to see the view from up there," Kai asks.

Milo grins and holds out his hand, which Kai takes without hesitation or a wince on her face.

Milo starts leading her upstairs.

"We'd love to see the view," Liesel cuts in, grabbing my arm.

We follow them up, and it takes everything in me not to rip Kai from Milo's arms.

Kai leans into his ear and whispers something, her eyes locked in an evil glare with mine.

I thought she got the hint when I fucked her in the bathroom and demanded she was mine, but apparently not.

Apparently, she'd rather cling to Mr. Boring here.

"It's beautiful," Liesel says when we reach the top, trying to barge in on Milo and Kai's romantic moment.

"You're beautiful," Milo says stroking Kai's cheek.

Really? Can the guy be any more cheesy?

We all stand in silence for a minute, watching the stars go by overhead.

"I have a surprise for you," Milo whispers to Kai, holding her in front of his body.

Liesel leans into me, but I don't think the jealousy thing is going to work with Milo. Not when he's so fascinated with Kai.

A firework starts to go off. And we all ooh and ahh.

"I thought the fireworks weren't supposed to go off until later?" Liesel asks.

Milo kisses the top of Kai's head. "I couldn't wait to show Kai."

I bet you couldn't wait.

I rub my neck as I stare up at the sparks in the sky. Other than tackling Milo, I have nothing left. I have no plan.

"Got anything?" I whisper to Liesel.

She shakes her head.

Fuck.

When I look up again, Milo is kissing Kai. His hand is on her ass, and she leans in as her eyes close like she's enjoying the kiss.

I lose it. I growl under my breath.

"Enzo, you can't make a scene," Liesel warns.

She's right. I see two men on the deck who I know are Milo's security. I don't have a weapon to defend myself. And I won't put Liesel nor Kai at risk.

Milo whispers something in Kai's ear, and she smiles brightly, her eyes hooded. And then I watch as they descend back down the stairs without a word or glance in our direction.

I've faced plenty of problems before, but none I couldn't solve or fix.

I'm not pissed because I'm going to lose this round.

I'm pissed because Kai kissed him.

I'm pissed because he's taking her to his private quarters.

And I'm pissed she's going to fuck him with my cum still inside her, all so she can beat me.

"Enzo? It's just a game. There will be other rounds. This is just the first battle. You can still win the war. The next round your father chose, and you know it will be better suited toward your talents."

I don't hear Liesel's words. They don't matter.

All that matters is that Milo is going to fuck Kai, and Kai is going to let him. *Did she play me this whole time? Can she touch other people without feeling pain?* Because I didn't think there was any way she was ready to hold another man's hand, let alone kiss or fuck him.

"Enzo, are you okay?" Liesel asks.

No, I'm not okay. Kai is about to fuck another man, and I can't stop it without getting us all killed. Because if she goes through with this, if she fucks that bastard, I'll kill them both. I'd rather die than let that bastard fuck her.

Come back to me, Kai. You're mine. And I'm not finished fucking you in every way possible. Come back, before he ruins you.

25

KAI

Kissing Milo is torture.

Every kiss burns my lips, my tongue, my mouth. Pain surges through my body with each slip of his tongue into my mouth. My heart slowly stops, trying to shut him out. My breathing is weak, and my body so cold.

"Are you cold, baby?" Milo asks.

Baby. Milo isn't allowed to call me baby, only Enzo is.

"A little," I say, shivering again.

He grins, his dimples deepening. "Don't worry; I'm about to warm you up."

His lips crash down on me again in a messy, sloppy kiss. He's been drinking, but I don't think he's drunk, just sloppy in comparison to Enzo.

It shouldn't make me feel guilty kissing Milo, not when Enzo kissed Liesel, but I do. I don't want to kiss Milo. I don't care about winning anymore, only surviving. I need to get off this yacht in one piece.

But I also want to punish Enzo and make him suffer for kissing Liesel after he fucked me.

I should be the only woman he kisses.

And he should be the only man I kiss.

Dammit, this stupid game.

Milo presses me hard into a door.

I wince as he fumbles with the door handle.

He doesn't notice my pain. No man other than Enzo ever has.

Finally, he gets the door unlocked, and we stumble inside.

I'm uneasy on my feet. The little amount of alcohol I've had makes me dizzy and lightheaded.

Milo shuts the door and panic rises in my chest. We are in a bedroom, his bedroom by the look of it. The bed is large, filling most of the room. There is a mirror on the ceiling and on the wall. *How many women has he brought here and fucked?* I don't want to be the next woman. *But how do I get out of this now?* First, I need to get the damn ring. Because if I leave now, the kissing him will all be for nothing.

"I could use another drink," I say, hoping more alcohol in both our systems will result in us passing out before he tries to get me to fuck him.

"Of course, anything you want," he grins at me. He locks the door he's standing in front of, his eyes already undressing me as he walks through a door at the back of the room.

I'm exhausted. I want to sit on the bed and get the pressure off my aching feet, but I don't want him to get any ideas that I want to move things to the bed.

He returns a minute later with champagne and a scotch.

I shake my head. He didn't even pay enough attention to me to realize I've been drinking scotch all night, not champagne.

"Here you go," he says holding out the flute glass to me.

I grab the scotch from his other hand and sip it.

He smirks at me. "You are the sexiest goddamn woman I've ever met."

I bat my eyelashes at him, trying to act like I'm turned on by his comment instead of disgusted.

I can do this. Just seduce him. Get the ring. And then get out before he tries to fuck you.

I glance around the room as I continue to sip the scotch. He takes my hand, and we sit down on the edge of the bed. I let my eyes drop to the ring again on his pinky finger. The key that will allow me to leave.

Being sexy will be the easiest way to steal the ring.

He leans down like he's going to kiss me on the lips again, but I grab his hand and instead kiss his palm and set my scotch on the floor. He does the same with the champagne glass.

I kiss him again, and his eyes glue to mine in a heavy terrifying way, because I know what that look means. He's planning all the ways he wants to fuck me.

I continue kissing his palm, stalling.

Do it.

I take his index finger in my mouth, and suck it like I'm sucking his dick instead of his finger.

He bites his lip as he holds in a growl from the sensation.

I force my lips to curl up in a smile as I move to his middle finger.

I get a small moan as my reward. *Disgusting*.

I give the same treatment to his ring finger as I push him hard in the chest making him fall backward on the bed.

I need to give him everything before I move to the last finger, the one with the ring I need to steal on it. Hopefully, the ring is loose and not tightly squeezing his finger, or I'll never get it off.

I keep his finger in my mouth as I force my legs to straddle him until I feel his erection.

I suck in a breath trying to keep my nerve.

I can do this. I'm so close.

But no matter what happens, I can't. *I can't fuck him. Not even to save my own life.*

I move my mouth to his last finger at the same time I ground my pussy over his dick. I take his pinky finger into my mouth.

His eyes roll back in his head, and he presses his erection deep inside me.

I feel sick.

As I pull my mouth off his finger, I bring the ring with me into my mouth.

The boat rocks hard in that moment, as if the sea is finally on my side.

"Oh my god! I think I'm going to be—"

I jump off of him and run to the door I hope leads to the bathroom. There is a small private hallway that leads to a bar and a bathroom. I duck inside, shut the door behind me, and then lock it.

I exhale deeply. My body is still wrecked with panic and anxiety from having to touch and kiss him.

Tears stream down my cheek.

I feel like a whore, and all I did was kiss him. I can't imagine how I would feel if I let things go any further.

I grab the ring from my mouth and stare at it. I smile gently; I got the ring. Now I just need to find a way out of here with my dignity intact.

A rattle at the door makes me jump.

"Kai? Are you okay?" Milo asks.

Shit.

I walk over to the toilet and flush. "Yes, I just get seasick sometimes," I say weakly.

I walk over to the sink and turn it on, pretending to wash my face. "I just need a minute to try and freshen up."

Hopefully the thought of me vomiting will turn Milo off.

I wait a few minutes, then turn the water off. I pinch my cheeks and loosen my hair to try and look more like a mess. Like I'm desperately ill.

Then I look at the ring I'm holding. I need a place to hide it. I can't wear it on my finger. I really only have one choice: my bra. I slip it inside, knowing if he does try and fuck me, he'll find the ring and discover my real intentions.

I slowly walk to the door, like I'm walking to my death. I unlock and open it.

Milo is standing with his arms on either side of the doorframe.

"Feel better?" he asks.

"Um...not really. I'm sorry, I think I just had too much alcohol, and I got seasick. I think some fresh air might help me feel better."

"Or lying down on my bed might help."

I smile weakly. "The fresh air is usually the most helpful."

I try to push past him, but he doesn't move. He glares down at me; his eyes still singular focused on eating my body.

"You don't get to tell me no, baby. No one tells me no."

"I'm sorry. How about a rain check? My breath reeks of vomit. And I don't want that to be the first memory we share together."

"I don't buy it."

"What?"

"I. Don't. Buy. It."

I shake my head.

"Plenty of women have tried it before. Seducing me, but not willing to give it up when the time comes. Hoping that by dangling me along, I will want you more and more. Until I make you my girlfriend in hopes of finally fucking you. It's not going to happen. Not unless your pussy is made of gold or something. I get what I want, and I want you. Now get the fuck on my bed. Naked. Ass up in the air because you're right—I won't be kissing you anymore."

"Fine, I just need air first." I'd rather throw my body overboard into the sea than let this sick fuck have me.

I duck under his arm, walking fast and with purpose toward the bedroom door. I get there before he does. I grab the handle and try to unlock it, but it doesn't unlock.

Fuck.

There is a keypad and screen on the wall.

"It doesn't unlock from the inside or outside without me entering that code first."

"You sick fuck."

He grins.

"Get on the bed."

"No."

He grabs my arm and throws me on the bed. *This can't be happening.*

He removes his tuxedo jacket as I clammer off the bed.

He grabs me again, and I slap him.

"A fighter, huh? I enjoy it more when you fight back."

I scream. "Help! Somebody, help me!" But I know my cries are useless. If his staff heard, they wouldn't come. And everyone else is upstairs listening to loud music. They won't hear me. Enzo might try and save me, but he might just as easily give me space thinking I'm safe and simply trying to steal the ring.

Fuck the ring.

I don't want it.

I'd give it to Enzo if he came and saved me.

Milo grabs my wrists and spins me around before I even have a chance to fight him. He holds my arms behind my back with one hand as he grabs my ass with the other.

"No! Please stop! Let me go," I cry, not caring the tears are falling. Let him see the pain he is causing me.

But my tears only make him harder. I need to stop begging for someone to save me and find a way to save myself.

Think!

A gun.

He has a gun. I'm sure of it. Langston said all dangerous men carry a gun. He showed me the most likely spots. I just need a free arm.

His sloppy mouth moves to my neck, and I let him. Moaning instead of pushing him away in fear.

"I said you would like it, baby. Just give into it. Stop fighting me," he whispers.

It's enough to get him to loosen his grip.

I slip one arm from his grasp and grab the gun from his waistband. I aim it at his heart.

"Get away from me. Now."

Milo grins, backing up. "You're a fiery one."

"I will shoot you if you touch me again. You can ask my husband; I'm a good shot."

He grins and glances down at the ring I'm wearing on the wrong finger. "I knew you were married. Something about you told me you were off limits."

"Then why did you come after me?"

"I like the married ones. The fighters. It's so much more fun this way."

I shake my head, disgusted by this man. I only thought he was a rich douchebag; I didn't realize he was a rapist.

"Unlock the door."

"Not without payment."

I freeze. "I'm not sucking your dick. And I'm not letting you fuck me. You will unlock the door if you still want your cock attached to your body." I aim the gun lower and ensure the safety is off.

"You know how to work a gun; I'll give you that. But are you strong enough to fire it?"

"I am."

He nods. "I have a feeling you are."

"Unlock the door. Now."

"Not without payment."

"I won't—"

He shakes his head. "I want the ring."

"What?" I panic. *Does he realize I stole his ring?*

He nods in the direction of the ring I'm wearing. "It means something to you. It's special. Something your husband gave you. If I can't have your body, then I want the ring."

I tremble. *He can't have the ring.* This ring is Enzo's. It's his mother's. It means too much to him. I can't just let him have it.

"The ring or you don't leave. *Ever.* I don't care if you kill me; you will never get out of this room alive. None of my staff have a way to override the door. You will be trapped in here forever if you kill me."

Fuck.

"The ring for your freedom."

I stare at the ring. *I will get you back. I promise.*

Carefully, I take the ring off. I toss the ring at him. He catches it.

"Good girl."

"Unlock the door."

He moves to the door, and I train the gun on him.

He starts to enter a code, and I hear the door mechanism unlocking. "Move away from the door," I say when he's finished.

I keep the gun on him as he moves away from the door, and I head to it. I try the handle, but it doesn't open. Words flash on the screen.

The door will unlock in twenty-four-hours.

Twenty-four-hours!

"What did you do?"

"I unlocked the door."

"No, you fucking didn't! Do you have a death wish? I will kill you."

"No, you won't." He walks closer to me until the gun is pressing against his chest.

He grabs the gun before I can react. *Why the hell didn't I pull the trigger?*

"You bastard."

He smirks. "I'm not a bastard. I unlocked the door as requested. You were the one who didn't confirm the details first before coming to an agreement. I'm a businessman, Kai. The key to winning is in the details. I unlocked the door; it just won't open for twenty-four-hours."

I tremble. I'm trapped with this bastard for twenty-four-hours.

"You won't fuck me. You promised."

"No, I won't fuck you, not until you beg me—which you will."

I cross my arms. "I think I can go twenty-four-hours without wanting to fuck an asshole."

He grins. "Not if I beat you for every second we are in here, only providing you with relief when you beg for my cock."

The first blow is always the hardest. It's the one that knocks you into reality. I never thought I'd get beaten on a yacht again. Never be trapped in a room while the ship rocks. But when Milo's fist flies into my chest, it all comes back.

The fear.

The agony.

The pain.

All of the memories consume me again. And I hate myself for falling victim again. There was a reason I hated boats. A reason I hated the water. Because you can't run from the monsters when there is nowhere to go.

26

ENZO

Kai has been gone for three fucking weeks.

When the yacht docked, she never got off. Langston, Liesel, and I waited in the car all night waiting for her to disembark. To see if she had the ring. If she had won.

But she never got off.

Every day that went by made me crazy.

What happened?

Did she get the ring?

Did she fuck him?

Did she get caught?

What happened?

Milo was photographed a day later giving some grand speech, without the ring.

So I knew she had it.

But where was she?

Then, the rumors started. Milo spread the word he'd fucked Enzo Black's whore and wife.

I hadn't told anyone I was married. I still wasn't sure if it was the right or wrong move entirely.

Milo broke the news to the world—and now he's my enemy.

I've been tracking him for weeks. But it doesn't seem Kai is still on board. Numerous other women have been brought on his yacht, but no sign of Kai.

Did she try to run from me when she had the chance?

"Sir," Langston says stepping into my office at my beach house.

"Have you found anything?"

"No."

"Keep fucking looking and don't come back until you have something." *How could she just disappear?* It's not possible. Not from my team with my resources.

At first, I was worried about Jarod's boss hunting her down. I've been tracking leads for weeks, trying to find out who owned Kai. Who controlled Jarod. And finally, I have my answer. And it's even more fucked up than I could imagine.

"What happens if we don't find her?" I ask Archard, who is sitting on the couch.

He opens his mouth to answer and then stops abruptly staring at my doorway like he's seen a ghost.

I turn in that direction, already knowing what I will see when I glance that way, but unsure of how I'll feel.

Relieved she is alright.

Pissed she has been gone so long.

Angry she fucked that monster.

Just as I knew she would be, Kai is standing in the doorway. Gone is the glamorous look she wore the last time I saw her. Now she wears yoga pants, an oversized sweatshirt, and baseball cap.

She walks into the room without a word or glance my way.

"The ring," she says, holding it out to Archard.

He takes it slowly from her hand and inspects it.

"I'm declaring Kai the winner of this round. I'll notify you both twenty-four-hours before the next round starts," Archard says before leaving the room like he can't get out of here fast enough.

"Tried to run and realized you couldn't, not without my help?" I say.

"No, I wasn't running. I just needed some time to think."

"I'm sure you did after what you did."

"What does that mean?"

"It means you didn't want to face me after you fucked him!"

She glares at me, giving me all of her hatred. But she has no right to be mad, not right now. Now I get to be pissed.

"Do you have any idea the damage you caused?"

Her mouth drops open at my words. "The damage I caused you? Are you serious?"

"Yes! You ruined my reputation. Black's reputation. You told him you were married to me, and then you fucked him. Repeatedly. He told the world he had stolen my whore, my wife. No one will think I can rule when I let my woman get taken from me so easily."

Her face reddens, and for the first time since I've known her, I don't think her skin would feel like ice if I touched her. It would be scalding like fire. Burning and torching my skin from her hatred from me.

"Why the fuck would you tell him we were married?"

"One; you never told me not to. But I didn't tell him."

"Then how did he figure it out?"

"The ring you gave me. He knew it was an engagement ring. He wanted to know whose it was. I couldn't come up with a lie, so I said you."

I stare down at her finger, searching for the ring she claims almost ruined me.

"Where is it?"

Her face goes white.

"Where. Is. The. Ring. Kai?"

"It's gone."

I raise an eyebrow. "You sold it?"

"Milo has it."

What. The. Fuck?

"Spreading your legs for him wasn't enough? You had to hurt me by giving him the only possession I care about?"

I see red. I've never been so angry. So out of control. I knock everything from my desk in one swoop just needing to be destructive. Then I grab the chair and fling it across the room. I want to hurt Kai like she hurt me.

There was no reason to sleep with Milo. No reason she could give that would make me understand how she could fuck me in the bathroom and then five minutes later fuck another man simply to win a game. No reason she could give to explain why she would give him the ring meant to protect her.

"You fucking whore!" I spit out.

"You sold me! You fucking sold me! Did you think I would be loyal to you? That just because you fucked me, I would never fuck another man?"

"Yes, you're mine! I thought I made that perfectly fucking clear."

"I'm nobody's, least of all yours!"

My body shakes from the adrenaline I'm feeling. Without thinking I grab her and push her against the wall. My lips crash down on hers, needing her to fucking know she's mine.

"Mine!" I cry as she fights me off from her lips. She

tastes as delicious as I remember, even though she betrayed me, my cock doesn't understand. He still wants her. I still want her.

But I can't have her. Not after she hurt me, again.

"I don't belong to any man. Let me go!"

"No, you're wrong. You belong to me. You had a choice, and you bet your life, all for a chance at getting answers from me. You lost, now live with it. You're mine."

"You fucking bastard. You don't want me; you just don't want anyone else to have me. You won't even let me go free."

"No."

"Who cares that I fucked him? Who cares that I gave him the ring? You don't care about me. You don't love me. Why does it matter?"

"Because you are mine."

I release her. I won't hurt her. Even though I want to. I won't touch her.

She betrayed me. Gutted me. She got in bed and spread her legs for a man I hate. Just to win a game. And then she stabbed me in the heart by giving him the ring. A ring I willingly gave her to protect her.

Unacceptable.

I will make her pay for what she did.

She wants her freedom from me. She will get it. But she will never truly be free. I'll make sure of that.

She hates being here; I'll make her wish she never begged me to let her free.

"Go," I say to her. "Shower, get rid of any remnants of Milo. Then I will let you know what your punishment is."

She doesn't fight me; she just leaves. But I doubt she will shower. She won't do anything to make me happy. Nothing to show I have any power over her.

She thinks I'm the devil. I'll show her how evil I can be.

I'll get my reputation back. And I'll retain my name—Black. Because she can't fight for the name if she isn't here to fight for it.

I pick up the phone and dial the number as a plan forms in my head.

I've been beyond nice to her.

I protected her.

I gave her everything she could ever want.

I even helped her in that bathroom by getting over her fear of being on that yacht.

And this is how she repays me—with her betrayal.

No more.

She thinks I'm the devil, so I will be. I'll release the man inside me my father spent years trying to cultivate. But once I release him, I can never go back. I'll grant her reprieve from me, but she won't ever be free. Because she will never stop thinking about me.

27

KAI

Why does this bedroom comfort me?

It shouldn't.

Enzo is a monster.

He made it even more clear downstairs in his office, when he accused me of fucking Milo. Or willingly giving up his mother's ring.

He thinks so little of me.

That I would betray him like that.

But I wouldn't.

I did everything I could to survive.

Something he will never understand.

It's been over an hour since Enzo dismissed me from his office. And this is where I came—his bedroom. *Our bedroom.*

The room where he held me captive.

The room where he taught me to sleep in a bed.

The room where I learned to love myself.

The room where he made me come with just his voice.

The room where he fucked me the first time.

The room where I healed.

I hug my legs to me, sitting in the middle of the bed, like this room can somehow fix everything.

It can't.

Any feelings I had for Enzo vanished.

I feel nothing.

I'm numb.

I'm broken.

I don't care about the game.

I don't care about winning.

I just want him to let me go. He can be Black; I don't want it. I've suffered enough.

The door opens, and Enzo steps inside with an eery calm to him.

I watch him with big eyes as he walks to the bed and sits down on his side, leaning back against the frame and stretching his long legs out in front of me.

"What are you doing?" I ask.

"I want to play a game."

"I'm tired of games."

"You are never tired of our truth or lies game."

I freeze. I don't want to play that game. I don't want to tell him the truth. I don't want to tell him how wrong he was downstairs. How badly he hurt me. But I can't keep it in. And I want to hurt him as badly as he wants to hurt me.

"Fine, you go first."

"You're a whore," he says.

I growl. "You did not just say that."

"Truth or lie, you're a whore," he repeats as plainly as if he were telling me the weather.

"Truth," I say, because that's what he thinks of me.

He waits for me to say something. Because apparently, this game is more about telling the truth than it is about concealing things from each other.

"I spent the last three weeks hiding," I say.

"Truth," he says almost bored.

Then he looks me dead in the eye. "I never sold you."

"Lies," I answer.

He opens his mouth to speak, but I stop him. I need to get my own truth out before he tries to hurt me with whatever comes next.

"Milo beat me."

"Lies," he says rolling his eyes.

I rip my hat and sweatshirt from my body, revealing the truth. I spent three weeks alone trying to heal so Enzo would never know what I suffered from Milo. So he wouldn't look at me as broken. But the damage Milo did couldn't be healed in three weeks.

My body is as purple and black as it was when I first arrived here after being held captive by Jarod. I'm broken. Milo only had me for twenty-four-hours, but he housed a rage I didn't think any man could.

"Kai," Enzo's voice breaks as he looks at me. And a silent tear drops down his cheek seeing the pain. Seeing what I went through. What I was desperate to stop from happening.

"He beat me because I wouldn't sleep with him. I wouldn't spread my legs and become the whore he wanted me to be."

Enzo winces when I say the word whore, realizing how stupid it was to call me that earlier. I can see the terror on his face at realizing how badly his words hurt me. Almost as badly as what Milo did to my body.

"And your mother's ring—it did save me in the end. It saved me from being raped. It was his payment, because he knew how badly it would hurt you, which in the end was all he wanted."

Sorrow fills his face in a way I've never seen before. Pain, agony, despair all flow through his veins.

"I didn't betray you. I never would. I did everything I could think of to keep him from touching me. To keep him from getting your mother's ring because even though you gave it to me to protect me, I knew how precious it was."

Silence.

There is nothing he can say to fix this. This can't be forgiven. Not easily, by either of us.

"You promised to protect me, and you did, with the ring. The bruises are nothing. I would have died if he had raped me. I couldn't have recovered. But he didn't, because of that ring."

My words hurt him, because whatever he came up here to say he still hasn't said it, and I know his words will be a betrayal of his own. He needed to get back at me, so he did. And I need to hear the monster he has become. Because despite all of it, I still want Enzo. His ring protected me. And that I can never stop thanking him for.

"Tell me," I say.

His eyes bug open. "I can't."

"Tell me what you came here to say."

"Fuck." He rubs the back of his neck and looks at me with tear stained eyes.

"I didn't sell you."

"You already said that."

He shakes his head. "I. Didn't. Sell. You."

"What?"

He takes my hand, and I pull it away. But he only grabs it again.

"I didn't sell you."

"But that's what the men said. I remember them saying your name when I was sold."

"That's what they wanted you to believe."

I frown. "Why did you hide the truth all this time? Why didn't you tell me you didn't sell me?"

"Because it was easier if you hated me. I wanted you to hate me. It was the only way I could protect you from the truth and keep you safe. Because if I didn't sell you, then someone else did. Someone would be looking for you and try to sell you again."

"Who?"

"I was wrong. No one is looking for you."

"Who. Sold. Me?"

He takes a deep breath and squeezes my hand like the next words are going to hurt.

"Your father."

I gasp; my face goes white.

"What? Why?"

He shakes his head. "Maybe he's crueler than either of us realized. Maybe he thought you were safer being sold rather than staying here and facing me. Maybe he thought he was toughening you up quickly rather than dealing with years of training. I don't know the answer, but he sold you."

I process his words. *My father sold me.*

It hurts beyond anything else, but it's not Enzo's fault. I can forgive him for the worst thing I thought he did to me.

I can forgive him.

And he can forgive me.

And we can move on as what...?

We still have to fight to become Black.

We still can't date.

We shouldn't be lovers.

It doesn't change anything.

We are still enemies.

My father sold me. Of all the things Enzo listed, the only

one that makes sense is he did it to toughen me up. To prepare me for what is about to come in these games. That's why I was never raped on that yacht. He couldn't bring himself to order those men to rape me, only break me. Push me to my limit.

It makes sense.

I turn back to Enzo who looks like he's about to be sick. When I'm the one who should be feeling this way.

"What else?" I ask.

He won't look at me. He's told two truths, which meant he was saving the worst truth for the end. *What truth could be worse than my father sold me?*

"Enzo, what was your third truth?"

"I'm so sorry. I thought you had betrayed me, hurt me. I thought you willingly fucked Milo. I thought you gave him the ring to hurt me. It killed me to think you were willing to fuck Milo to win a stupid game. It broke my damn heart."

"I didn't though." And Enzo can't have feelings for me. It's not possible. I'm just a possession to him. Not someone who could hurt him.

"I did."

I frown. "You did what? You fucked Liesel?"

He shakes his head, and I can breathe again. For some reason that would hurt me. Him fucking another woman would kill me as badly as my father's betrayal.

"Then what?"

"I sold you."

"But you just said…"

"I didn't sell you before. But I sold you now, to Milo. He's coming in an hour, and I'm not sure I can stop him."

The End

282

Thank you so much for reading! Enzo and Kai's story continues in Trapped by Lies!

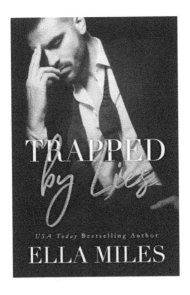

Want to order signed paperbacks? Visit: store. ellamiles.com

FREE BOOKS

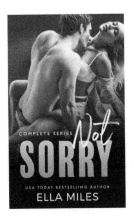

Read **Not Sorry** for **FREE**! And sign up to get my latest releases, updates, and more goodies here→EllaMiles.com/freebooks

Follow me on BookBub to get notified of my new releases and recommendations here→Follow on BookBub Here

Join Ella's Bellas FB group for giveaways and FUN & a **FREE** copy of **Pretend I'm Yours**→Join Ella's Bellas Here

ALSO BY ELLA MILES

TRUTH OR LIES (Coming 2019):

Lured by Lies #0.5

Taken by Lies #1

Betrayed by Truths #2

Trapped by Lies #3

Stolen by Truths #4

Possessed by Lies #5

Consumed by Truths #6

DIRTY SERIES:

Dirty Beginning

Dirty Obsession

Dirty Addiction

Dirty Revenge

Dirty: The Complete Series

ALIGNED SERIES:

Aligned: Volume 1 (Free Series Starter)

Aligned: Volume 2

Aligned: Volume 3

Aligned: Volume 4

Aligned: The Complete Series Boxset

UNFORGIVABLE SERIES:

Heart of a Thief

Heart of a Liar

Heart of a Prick

Unforgivable: The Complete Series Boxset

MAYBE, DEFINITELY SERIES:

Maybe Yes

Maybe Never

Maybe Always

Definitely Yes

Definitely No

Definitely Forever

STANDALONES:

Pretend I'm Yours

Finding Perfect

Savage Love

Too Much

Not Sorry

ABOUT THE AUTHOR

Ella Miles writes steamy romance, including everything from dark suspense romance that will leave you on the edge of your seat to contemporary romance that will leave you laughing out loud or crying. Most importantly, she wants you to feel everything her characters feel as you read.

Ella is currently living her own happily ever after near the Rocky Mountains with her high school sweetheart husband. Her heart is also taken by her goofy five year old black lab who is scared of everything, including her own shadow.

Ella is a USA Today Bestselling Author & Top 50 Bestselling Author.

Stalk Ella at:
www.ellamiles.com
ella@ellamiles.com